LIFE IN THE SHADOWS

Emily Tallman

Visit our website at www.StillwaterPress.com for more information.

First Stillwater River Publications Edition

ISBN-10: 1-946-30044-6
ISBN-13: 978-1-946-30044-7

1 2 3 4 5 6 7 8 9 10
Written by Emily Tallman.
Cover design by Nathanael Vinbury.
Published by Stillwater River Publications, Pawtucket RI, USA.

Publisher's Cataloging-In-Publication Data
(Prepared by The Donohue Group, Inc.)

Names: Tallman, Emily.
Title: Life in the shadows / by Emily Tallman.
Description: First Stillwater River Publications edition. | Pawtucket RI, USA : Stillwater River, [2018]
Identifiers: ISBN 9781946300447 | ISBN 1946300446
Subjects: LCSH: Mentally ill women--Fiction. | Paranoia--Fiction. | Grief--Fiction. | LCGFT: Psychological fiction. | Paranormal fiction. | Thrillers (Fiction)
Classification: LCC PS3620.A5377 L54 2018 | DDC 813/.6--dc23

DEDICATIONS

This work is dedicated to my mother who ever patiently supported me when I left full time work to follow my dreams and who was there to tell me when work I thought was done could be better. She reminds me every day how excited she is to hold a copy in her hands and open the cover to see her daughters face. There is no motivation more powerful than a mother's love.

I would also like to thank my friends for understanding when I would drop off the radar for weeks at a time while writing and to Jen Jacobs the most. Without your amazing generosity, this series would have never left scribbles in a notebook. Thank you so much for giving me your support in the form of my beautiful laptop that I will cherish forever.

I love you.

I try to stay asleep, I really do, but it's hard to stay in bed with eyes boring into the back of your skull.

I can feel the spot it's looking at sticking out of the blankets, feel the cold stare press against me like the barrel of a gun. I can't go back to sleep but I can't leave my safe little cave of quilts either. If I don't look, I can't see it. My mind circles around the pros and cons in that idea.

Pro, I think to myself, it could all be a part of my imagination or an echo from a nightmare.

Con, what is it doing that I can't see? And if I look, it would know I am awake and I would see it and it would see me seeing it and isn't that how the climax of a lot of horror movies start?

I swallow hard around a dry mouth and throat and curl in on myself. I hear a rustle, it was moving closer. I close my eyes as tight as I can, letting tears slip out, and try to cover the cold spot on my head without being too obvious. I take a deep breath.

It takes a deep breath. A haunted, hollow, dragging breath that clicks at the start and finish.

Mechanical.

Evil.

Not human.

Not like my quick, shaky gasps.

And if I could hear it breathing then it must be close, right by the bed. Waiting. A silent sob shakes me, moving the blanket further down my head and shoulders.

I open my eyes.

CHAPTER ONE

If happiness and optimism are said to be a mind looking through rose colored glasses then depression is a shroud. A heavy thing blurring your world, making it that little bit darker. It muffles sound, weighs on your neck and gives it those twinging stabs of pain until you give in and walk with your head bowed. Until you're always looking down and never really noticing the simple beauty happening in the everyday world around you.

Life goes on and you forget there was ever anything light and beyond your heavy veil until something grabs your attention. Something makes you look up or listen or feel. That something can be a lifting force, something to pull you up, something to give you fresh air, new life... or something to make you see how low you've come, add another few inches, a few pounds to that shroud. Close you in just a bit more.

For me, that something is a laugh.

I sit in the corner of a tiny café, the end of my block being easier to walk to than the grocery store to get more tea and maybe, if I was feeling up to it, a little bit to eat. I'm not. The sugar crusted top of my still warm blueberry muffin shines untouched. I pick at the receipt stuck to my plate. Olivia is scrawled across it. I tear it off and crumple it in my fist feeling the sharp points of paper poke at my palm. I had said my name clearly, spelt it and everything. "Livia. L-I-V-I-A." I hate my name, hate Olivia even more.

Grief. It consumes me, sucking the life from my bones and shrouding all of my senses in a veil of chilly, washed out evening blue even though it is barely ten AM.

1

The smell of the café, a smell I once loved and kept with me in scented candles and the sheer amount of coffee I had brewed during college and into my working life, is now turning my stomach. Things change. This place has changed. I wonder what the little old lady who used to own it would think of what has become of the place. It looks so different now. Not the cozy book café it used to be back when I was in college. Not the quiet, dusty spot with over frosted cupcakes and too sweet drinks I used to hide away in when Nick or life in general was too much to handle. It's modern now. "Grindhouse" is spelled out in rusted and paint splotched metal over the main counter. The old mismatched shelving units and Salvation Army chairs and couches have been replaced with faux brick walls and industrial wood and metal tables and chairs. As masculine now as the place used to be little old cat lady feminine. Lit posters of gory movies decorate the walls and show-time flyers are posted in the windows. Couches full of students are huddled around an unlit movie screen in the back, the faint smell of popcorn still lingers under the constant onslaught of coffee.

I hate the smell of freshly ground beans and boiling caffeine for reasons I don't want to think about. I'm ready to get up and go, to leave the nearly ten dollar treats and go back to hiding in my empty apartment like I'm waiting out a war, but then I hear it. The laugh. Well, if such an extraordinary sound could have so simple a name as *laugh*.

It is this luminescent, thick, stunning blast of sound that booms through the swinging doors to the kitchen. It drowns out the droning crowd and grinding machines and even the dulcet tone of some slow singing someone or other of the day from the speakers above. It stops me dead. I'm stuck, hovering between sitting and standing, not knowing what I'm feeling or recognizing this unknown emotion that is tearing through me. But it sure is something, and I know it can keep me coming back even if I can't bring myself to eat or drink.

I'm stuck, hovering between sitting and standing, not knowing what I'm feeling or recognizing this unknown emotion that is tearing through me. But it sure is something, and I know it can keep me coming back even if I can't bring myself to eat or drink.

I once knew laughter like that, knew the sound of my own awkward gasping and snorting that would immediately send others into hoots of their own at my expense. Something in-

2

side me craves it so strongly it has my legs shaking and me falling back into my chair to soak it in and catalogue the layers of the sound. The tone and vibrations of it wash over me, relaxing and stretching each muscle and ache. I feel it cradle me and think that I can just close my eyes and let it lull me into a perfectly dreamless sleep for the first time in months.

When the sharp creak of a door swinging open makes me jump, I snap open eyes I didn't realize I have actually closed in public. They dart to find the still chuckling figure without thought, like my body is acknowledging and accepting something my mind isn't quite ready for.

Flour and something else, something bright like maybe smooshed blueberries or raspberries is smeared across one dark cheek. There is a shock of sunny exhilaration on his strong features, curved lips and smiling bright eyes. My eyes sting with the same brilliant pain as looking into the sun after spending hours under heavy covers. He is a screaming white wall of light in a dark movie theater. My breath catches in a way that makes me dizzy. I would have rolled my eyes and fake gagged at anyone else had it not just happened to me. I can't look away from this blinding man, demanding of attention. Maybe the twinging pain isn't in my eyes. It definitely isn't enough to make me stop staring.

The sound is better when I can see it bubble up from somewhere inside of him to escape into the air, pushing away the fog and bringing bright clarity. It is even better to see the crinkles around his eyes, the expanse of throat and dancing Adam's apple, unguarded, unconcerned, unthreatened. It's better than the sound somehow. And yet worse to know how much I could miss something so... genuine and everyday as a laugh.

It feels like I've been drugged. At least I know it isn't the coffee. I had only swirled a tea bag in my hot water, watching the leaves' color spread and stain the surface. I had never gotten around to actually taking a sip.

I watch the man go about setting fresh muffins and scones in the display case and head back to the kitchen to talk animatedly to someone inside before I gather up my purse and uneaten food to head back out into the chilly fall day. The wind bites my cheeks and tugs my hair over my eyes the whole way

3

home, but I can't bring myself to care. I squish the bottom of the muffin between my fingers and wonder if I should have asked for a bag before seeing one of the city's many homeless and deciding to pass it on instead of letting it probably go rock hard in my kitchen. I'm sure it would have been delicious, I'm just not in the mood to eat anymore.

CHAPTER TWO

"**Y**ou respect my space and I'll respect yours. If not, I swear to whoever your god is, I will end your disgusting existence." I grumble as I watch the spider who has skittered into my shadow on the wall before freezing to wriggle its two front legs at me. It better not be one of the jumping ones. It's a tiny thing. Not a baby, but definitely not the thick, hairy adult it could have been. I'll let the spider live out its teenage dreams in peace. As long as I don't find it in my bed later.

Bed = Dead.

Getting out of bed to clean my room and go for a walk was exhausting enough, let alone the little emotional journey I had just experienced in the coffee shop. Grabbing a shoe to show a spider who is at the top of this food chain isn't really on my list of priorities at the moment. If I can't be bothered to go grocery shopping or even eat something besides the little snacks stashed under my bed, then a spider barely even registers. The only reason I'm even in the bathroom is to self-consciously brush my teeth. I had been too lazy before leaving the apartment and my anxiety is reeling at the thought that such a glorious person as the baker of The Grindhouse Café may have wanted to talk to me while I had rank breath. Not that this happened or ever would, but my irrational fears don't quite understand that.

I spit the minty foam out into the sink and straighten back up to lash my pearly could-be-whiters in the mirror. The spider is moving in the corner of my eye again, but it's moving away so I put it out of my mind. What I can't ignore, however, is that my shadow is no longer against the wall.

5

"That's strange." I look up to make sure a bulb hasn't burned out and shift my body back and forth, watching the shadow draped across the wall behind me in the mirror. It never moves next to me where it had been hiding the spider before. I have a weird sense of déjà vu and turn off the lights to head back to my room. "Déjà vu really isn't needed today, I've had a long enough few hours as it is." I tell the universe.

I try to gather up clothes for a wash, but that tickle of remembrance is making the phone in my pocket burn hot and heavy. I think I may want to listen to my psychiatrist for once and that this might be the best time to start. I'm already a bit emotional, it's not like it could get worse. Or at least, not worse than I'd faced in the last few months.

*****

"Hey! You've reached Nick Savage. I'm probably tearing my place apart looking for this phone so shout for me and I'll ring ya back when I find it."

I try to compose myself, it's been so long since I've heard his voice, even his cheery phone voice. The automated female asks me to record a message after the tone or press one for more options. If life were only as simple as pressing a button for more ways fate's script could turn out. I have time for one more sniffle before the beep.

"Hey Nick. Uh..." I shake my head, why am I even calling again? Acceptance, forgiveness, moving on? Blah blah shrink talk blah? The burn and pressure of tears builds up behind my eyes just saying his name but it's too late now, I'm being recorded here, I have to pull it together and get to the point. Dr. Baron said it would help, but it just feels like delaying the inevitable. "I just really needed to hear your voice today. I miss you." I say, having to pause and take a deep breath. My head spins and it feels like I haven't really breathed in years. "God, I... I don't even know what's happening. I think I'm going crazy. I'm scared and I don't know what to do. I need you."

The beep sounds again, letting me know I'm out of time and signals the building tears to fall and the sobs to rake my lungs raw. Just that tiny bit of his voice breaks something inside of me again. Calling was a horrible idea.

This is a low. I'm at the point where I'm ready to flop back on the bed I finally had the energy to remake after a week of only leaving it to use the bathroom across the hall or binge on whatever was left in the cupboards. I try deep, calming breaths but for some reason all I can hear echoing in my mind is a laugh. Not the perfect, booming blessing from earlier, but Nick's.

Nick's laugh was anything but kind. The last time I had heard the sound it had been a punch. The bright sharpness of it like glittering glass before it cuts you. I should have known then.

It could have been the comforter puffing up when I collapse back down or maybe a piece of mail falling off the desk, but I could swear something moved in the corner of my eye again.

I check the room, but I'm alone. I try to control my breathing, but that's a joke because it was already too fast and not enough at best after that torturous call. I slide off of the bed.

There used to be a gun in the nightstand Nick had insisted on when I had first moved in, but I don't bother looking for it now. I know my brother hid it when he moved out. Ted is overprotective like that. He doesn't trust me not to hurt myself with it but doesn't trust my ability to defend myself without it either. Not knowing where it is doesn't help protect anyone. There is an aluminum bat from my community softball days in the hall closet, but I doubt it will do any good. I don't really want it to, if that makes sense. It wouldn't be the only thing that doesn't make sense right now.

"It doesn't matter because it was nothing", I have to tell myself if I'm ever going to be brave enough to enter the dark hallway.

I clench my fist around my cell phone, just in case, and creep to the bedroom door, barely poking my head out to look down the hall both ways.

Nothing but darkness. I can't hear anything that would suggest someone else being there, just my own harsh pants for breath dragging in and out. It was probably just a "floater" or whatever the eye doctor had called the little splotches my mother could see in the corner of her vision from time to time. But something still feels wrong. Like someone is watching me from within the darkness.

Dread runs its icy fingers down my spine as I reach forward to feel against the wall as far as I can reach without moving too far ahead into the black.

The light switch pinches my thumb as I flip it up and illuminate a figure just a few feet away.

I whip my hand back to my chest and slam backwards against the doorframe, opening my mouth in a silent shocked scream. I blink into the new light and it's gone. It wasn't there. Wasn't real. It couldn't have been. "I did not just see that. I did not just see that." I repeat to myself, hand still over my pounding heart. The thought that I could have was too dizzying to comprehend.

I don't know how long I stand there frozen, staring into the empty hallway. Nothing is there but my own shadow draped across the floor and bottom of the wall in front of me. I finally back carefully into my bedroom again and close the door tightly. A last second burst of adrenalin has me moving anything on the floor (shoes, a sweater, a stuffed rabbit, more shoes, why were so many shoes on the floor?) in front of the door and backing up further to the bed.

And then it hits me. I have time to take a lung bursting breath before I'm laughing hysterically. Dark, rusty sounds leaving me. It's nowhere near my old laugh, but it's refreshing none the less. "I just pissed myself over my own shadow! I'm going crazy. What the hell is wrong with me?" I question the empty room, expecting no answer but the silence and secretly hoping no answer would come. I crawl back onto the bed. "Screw today."

I take a moment to contemplate the prescription bottles on the nightstand. Livia Moss. 229 B Cyprus Avenue, Boston, MA. I shake my head around another huff of tear tinted laughter. "What good are they?" I whisper. I know what they're for, why I should continue to take them. Migraines, sleeplessness, depression, anxiety, and hypervigilance. But none of them feel right, feel like me. It's like I am just a hollow version of my old self. Emotionless, overly energetic to the point of exhaustion when I take them. They weren't right. I would rather feel the guilt. Nothing took away the darkness or fear. At least without the foggy minded state the prescriptions prompted, I am present enough to know why I'm in such a down place for the first time in so long.

I may have been doing nothing but sleep for days but it's all of a sudden obvious that I still need more. My hand stops halfway to pulling the light chain on the ceiling fan before I think better of it and snuggle into the pillows instead, pulling half the comforter I'm laying on over myself, not even bothering to get all the way into the bed.

*****

The light blaring through the window wakes me up and all of a sudden it's like I've gone back in time to when I would wake naturally and happy with the sun and not close out nature and all sense of time with closed blinds and heavy shades. I sit up and I stretch, letting the odd thought slip from my mind as I pop all of my joints perfectly and crawl out from between the expensive sheets and fluffy blankets. Nick always kicks to them the floor during the night but I can't sleep without them. I shuffle down the hall into the kitchen and pause to look at something on the floor. The line of the rug touching the kitchen tiles is a funny color. Like someone spilled something and didn't clean it properly.

"Men." I mumble to myself as I turn on the coffee machine. The glass pot is missing. I look around the counter and over at the kitchen table to see where Nick could have left it but it's nowhere in sight. His keys are still on the counter, where is he? A cool shower would have to suffice over caffeine this morning.

I pull back the shower curtain and turn the faucet on, letting the spray wash over my arm to test the temperature. Something is sticking to the fine hairs there, matting them to the skin and shining dully under dust and lint from a night's sleep. I let the water run over it some more before shaking off my hand and turning around to get a towel from the cabinet under the sink. Everything stops when I see the mirror.

There is something behind me.

A massive, dark shape. Like a person wearing a black cloak. There was no face. I gasp and turn around, heart ready to explode out of my chest with its frantic pumping but there was nothing there. I turn back and see the shadow again. It's turning back around too.

Left, left.

Right, right.

It moves with me like it knows what I'm thinking, what I'm about to do, where I will run. It's terrifying and somehow hypnotic. I raise my fist to throw at the glass, but it too is draped in the same darkness. I look down and my body is in the same cloth. It's not possible. Something inside me calms even as I claw and scream to escape.

The shape in the mirror is me.

*****

My eyes fly open to see the scroll ceiling of my bedroom in the apartment. I gasp in a few breaths, my hands still clawing at the blanket wrapped around me, desperate for an escape. I slowly unclench my hands from the tangled thing to look at them.

No shadow. No mysterious draped cloth.

Just clipped nails, dry knuckles and a few freckles. I drop my hands back down to rest on my legs as they flex with left-over nerves from the dream. Just a dream.

More like a nightmare.

The light of a new day slips through the blinds and mixes with the harsher yellow light from the ceiling fan. I slide my eyes closed again but my heart is still beating a little too fast and everything is too bright. I take a few deep breaths and try to slip into a better dream anyway. I'm almost there when I notice the hum in the air.

My eyebrows furrow as I listen. It sounds like the noise a television makes when you mute it. My tired mind tries to figure out how long I've left the TV on and what the bill would be between that and my recent habit of sleeping with the lights on. I prop myself up to find the remote and look to the corner where the old thing is propped precariously on half a shelf and half of my desk (aka mail and unfolded laundry pile up center), but something is blocking my view.

Sitting on the corner of the bed, right by my feet in a beam of dusty sunlight from the window like an incredibly large and creepy but content housecat, is a shadow.

It turns its faceless head to look at me and everything inside me freezes again to just stare back.

I'm sweating and shaking and definitely oxygen deprived but no part of me can possibly move. I can't even blink. It hasn't disappeared yet and it definitely isn't in any way my shadow. It's short and thin and hunched and *just not me.*

I finally find it in myself to give my lungs reprieve and breathe. The shadow is still there.

I blink. Still there.

I muster up all the courage I can to trust this is some kind of lingering dream and close my eyes to rub at them.

Still there.

"Okay. Either I'm not crazy or I'm *extremely* crazy." The shadow raises its head at my words as if listening, the ebbing darkness moving in front of its face like shifting fabric. "Yeah… pillow room for me. That's okay I like pillows." *Fight fear with humor*, I think to myself, *that's the way to fix the problem.* It stands up slowly and that is not okay. *Jokes and sarcasm cannot fix monsters moving closer!* "Stop! Don't move!" I shout, panicking. It listens. I take the opportunity to quickly stumble off the bed and stand with my back safely against the wall.

I do my best to keep my hand up and outstretched in the uniform motion for 'stop' but what I hope is broadcasting through the tremors is some variation of *'don't you dare even think about twitching'* before I decide I have the nerve to yell at a hallucination for a second time.

"Leave! Get out!" The thing sits back on the bed and my heart dips down into my stomach in another fearful round of *what do I do now?* before the thing disappears.

No poof.

No smoke.

Just gone.

I'm alone. I definitely feel alone right now.

When I manage to focus the full blown hyperventilation into more normal breathing with panic trembles subdued but ready to get right back into gear under my skin, I bring myself to sit down again.

I pick up my phone, go into the emergency contacts and hit *Ted*. Two rings in and I can hear my brother's signature aggravated chuff and some girlish giggling in the background. "Really bad timing Liv, call you later."

The call ends and before I even realize what I'm doing, my fingers are scrolling through my list of favorites.

"Hey! You've reached Nick Savage. I'm probably tearing my place apart looking for this phone so shout for me and I'll ring ya back when I find it."

All I have the strength to do is pull my knees up to my chest, push end, and cry.

Chapter Three

If I had been in hell before, then I'm in a whole new circle now. Every little thing makes me jump and on more than one occasion I've found myself pressing my back to the nearest wall and having a seemingly untriggered panic attack. I can't be in a room with a closed off portion big enough to hide someone without the irrational fear that something is there that I can't see. I will fall asleep after hours of staring at my closet, flinching awake at the smallest of sounds. My eyes will dart around the room searching for an intruder in the light from the TV I have taken to using as a night light on the nights when I can't bear to be in complete darkness. Reaching up into the unknown to tug the ceiling light back on can seem impossible. And where I once couldn't sleep without the fresh air from the hall way, I now can't even dream of relaxing with the bedroom door open. I'm showering with the curtain open, ruining the ugly generic apartment linoleum. What am I? A claustrophobic, agoraphobic combination plate?

After a few days it gets to the point where I have moved the case of water and a box of cookies from the kitchen to my bedroom so if I get hungry I won't have to leave my fortress. If nature calls during the night I wait until daytime lights the little apartment before running the five feet across the hall to the bathroom.

When Thursday rolls around, it has been six days since the last time I had gone outside. Considering my ever present battle with depression and more recent diagnosis of post-traumatic stress and hypervigilance, the recent manic behavior isn't exactly something unusual. But I have to leave tomorrow. If I have ever needed to speak with my work-mandated therapist, now was the time.

I pick at the broken pieces of Nutter Butter at the bottom of the package and look down at my rumbling stomach. First step would have to be the kitchen. The probably empty kitchen, but I would have to hope the things creeping in the corner of my eye decided to make me a lasagna and leave it in the fridge.

No such luck. But there was yogurt that had magically not passed its expiration date in the almost month I haven't been to the store and some freezer bagels. There were other frozen things stored away in there too, but right now I would need to make a combination of them and it was just too much effort. Yogurt would do until I could go shopping on my way home tomorrow.

I make a mental grocery list while polishing off the chocolate mousse and cherry cobbler flavored yogurt. They go surprisingly horrible together. I creep my way nervously back to my bedroom to set my alarm and find something on television boring enough to maybe make me go to bed at a semi-decent hour tonight.

Ten hours later, I reenter the land of the living but feel no need to immediately vacate the warm flannel sheets and quilts pulled up over my head. I haven't slept in such a sheets-off-the-corners nest in years. It's nice, but something still feels wrong. Not the *'these are flannel sheets, not Nick's ridiculously priced ones'* or the *'the body pillow against my back feels nothing like an actual living, breathing person'* wrong that I had been facing lately. It feels more like someone is watching me. I let out a shaky sigh and pull back the covers, looking at the visible half of the room. Nothing. I don't know why a cold sweat is gluing the old T-shirt to my back but something has me turning slowly to check out the other side of the room. And, nothing. Just the closed door and make-shift barricade of shoes I had taken to piling in front of it at night.

I sit up, pull my knotted hair into a quick, messy bun and turn on the TV. I glance at the alarm clock by my bed while flicking through the channels, ten forty. *Not exactly the witching hour* I think to myself. One hour until I have to think about getting ready for my appointment with Dr. Baron, ten minutes before my alarm clock will go off.

I browse through the channels trying to find something to entertain myself before I have to leave my little nest. I can see my hollow eyed reflection staring back at me in the brief seconds of blackness before each new channel kicks in. Something about it has a stone weighing heavy in my stomach and the cold sweat picking back up again. I'm probably getting sick. Perfect timing.

Talk show, reflection, Shopping Network, reflection, Telemundo... something feels wrong. I should probably eat. The Cooking Network is next and acts as a sign. I turn off the television again and start kicking off the sheets, looking at the dark screen with the pale face staring back. I'm about to get lost in how much I have changed these past few months and an internal battle on whether or not to schedule an appointment to tame my hair when I see something move on the left of the screen.

I feel my brow furrow as I lean forward. If it was that spider from the bathroom, it could say goodbye. But no, as I get closer the barely there shape moving around takes form. A dark shape, like my shadow if I had been standing, reaches out a hand to me. I gasp at the intruder and fling myself off the bed to face him.

But there's no one. Just something moving in the corner of my eye. I stand up and whirl around again, but I'm alone. I crawl back into the sheets and tug them down around me, just my eyes peeking out to scan the room like a child who thinks their comforter is the top line of defense against a monster in the closet. There's nothing.

"What the hell?" This is not okay. Goosebumps rise beneath the sweat dripping down the back of my neck and I can feel it, that heaviness in the air like I'm sharing it with countless others and then I see that little movement, that something hovering just out of my line of sight. My eyes dart to the left, trying to chase the shadow but it's too fast. I shoot up out of bed, adrenalin pumping through my veins, there is something that I can't see and I will be damned if I ever let anyone or anything sneak up on me again. Could hallucinations even do this? *Wasn't the point of seeing things that weren't there that you could actually SEE them?*

This feels like proof somehow, like some kind of validation that I'm not paranoid, that I'm not afraid for no reason. Those things I saw, they were real, lurking just beyond my frame of vision and ready to pounce. But it also kind of confirms that I'm seeing things, "Not to repeat myself or anything, but *what the hell?*

"Show yourself! Where are you, you bastard?" I scream so loud I think my throat will bleed. "Where the hell are you?" I start sobbing again, from fear or exhaustion or frustration I can't tell. The tears sting and well in my eyes and darkness starts to form at the corners of them but when I whip my head around there is still nothing. I start to yell again, words broken and garbled around my tears, "What do you want from me!" I feel something brush against me, a cold tingle like static or a draft tickling the hair on the back of my neck. I turn around and around frantically but I am alone. I need to get out, get away from this place. It doesn't matter where. I wrench the door open, shoving the shoes out of the way to fling myself into the hall and there it is.

There *they* are.

Left, right, front, five, six, a dozen shadows are crowded into my tiny hallway, their attention on me. The tears stop falling on my face, frozen like me with fear at the realization that this is so much more real and terrifying than anything I could prepare for. Something inside me breaks. I feel it slide out of place as I silently back into my room again. I close the door and keep backing up until the bed knocks at my knees. "I can't." I hear myself say, not planning the words. My feet feel exposed on the floor like one of those things might pull me down under the bed. I lift them up and hug my knees, chin digging into the muscles of my thighs as I stare at the door and wait. I'm not sure what for. Why are they here? They must be about to do something. Bust in, kill me, whatever real life monsters do.

The alarm clock behind me blares and sends my heart into another dizzying whirl of frantic beats. It's a moment before I have the presence of mind to make the decision to look away from the door and reach for the clock to switch it off. "I can't." I say again. What do I do? I can't go back into that hallway, can't leave. I'm trapped here. I need help but who do you call for this? The little, childish part of me stripped bare and hanging by the last floss thin thread of life's rope whispers *Ghostbusters!* but I can't even blink at my own joke. I reach for my phone and scroll through the contacts for Dr. Baron. This is what she's here for, right? This is the shit I'm paying for… maybe. That's what I'm going to go with at least. Hallucinations are slightly less scary than whatever the hell else right now.

"Dr. Wilks and Dr. Baron's office. Sharon speaking." I pause for a moment. What could I even say? How do you approach full on crazy like this? Was that even what this was? What if Dr. Baron came over for a house visit and was mauled by these things? "Hello? Dr. Wilks and Dr. Baron's office. This is Sharon."

"Hi." It's all I can manage. Maybe this was shock. I've felt that before, where I didn't talk, couldn't talk for over a week. If that's the case, then *hi* was a pretty good start.

"Yes, hello, can I help you?" Yes, that's what I need, help. I just had to ask now. Another good step. I swallow.

"Hi, I'm Livia. A patient of Dr. Baron's. I need to speak with her."

"I'm sorry she can't take phone calls right now. Can I take a message?"

"I…" what can I say? No? Can I do that? "I really need to speak with her."

"I'm sorry but you can't. I can have her call you back though." The girl's smiley voice seemed to be losing its patience.

"I need to cancel my appointment. Livia Moss. It was at one o'clock. And I need to reschedule for tomorrow and I really need her to call me back."

"I'm sorry but if you cancel, we are fully booked. You won't be able to reschedule for a few weeks. But your next appointment is still on for two weeks from today. You should get a call sometime after five if that's alright?"

"Why that long? Can't you give her the message now?" The girl, Sharon, sighs and I have to catch myself from sighing twice as loud down the crackly line. She thinks her day is hard, she could come right over and try her luck at staying sane.

"Dr. Baron is busy with patients today."

"Well can't she call at one since I won't be there? I'll pay for my hour, we can do it by phone. Please."

"I'm sorry, we can't do that. Are you alright, hun? Do you need me to call someone for you?" *Yeah, my psychologist!* My inner monologue rages. *How many times do I need to say it?*

"I just need to talk to Dr. Baron." I can feel my throat tightening with that hopeless, bottomless fear again. I was either going to start yelling or crying very soon.

"I will give her your message. If it's an emergency, please consider dialing 911." She says and hangs up. I lock my phone and stare down at it for a moment. Maybe I should have said something more, but what could I say? I make up my mind to try calling back at one.

That cold static feeling dances across my arm and I look up to see the small shadow again. It's sitting on the foot of my bed, barely two feet from me. I freeze, can't speak, can't cry. I use the last of my strength to shuffle back against the headboard and pick up the phone again. I don't need to look at it to enter my password or find Nick's number in the favorites. I bring it to my ear just in time to hear the end of a ring and, "Hey! You've reached Nick Savage. I'm probably tearing my place apart looking for this phone so shout for me and I'll ring ya back when I find it."

CHAPTER FOUR

The week to follow passes much like the first, in fear, paranoia, and loneliness. Dr. Baron never calls. I leave a message every day until it's Thursday again and still nothing. I didn't understand how a psychiatrist chosen by the hospital I work for could have so little interest in keeping up with clients. Isn't her entire job to care about things and people when no one else will? To listen? To help? Or was it just to report to her patient's employers regarding whether or not they are a sane employee fit for work? How does Dr. Baron know I'm sane and ready to go back if she wouldn't see me during my most insane moments?

I try to call my brother to see if, when he was living in the apartment, he had ever seen anyone or anything and he gets worried. Worried enough to come over with Chinese food and sodas. I tell Ted about everything I have been seeing, about how afraid I am here. Ted just looks at me with sad eyes and tells me that I have always had an over active imagination. He thanks me for wasting his time on what was supposed to be a date night before he leaves. We used to be best friends.

It was nice to have it confirmed that I am indeed, a waste now.

I try to take pictures with the camera on my phone to send to him, to prove to the person I thought would always be there for me that I'm right, that I still need him and am important enough to make time for. Every time the things would either disappear before I could open the camera app or not show up in the pictures at all. This should probably count as proof that I'm crazy and not haunted. I start a list.

First, they do not show up in photographs.

Second, now that I've seen them, I can't unsee them. They are everywhere and if one leaves, another would soon take its place as if I am under surveillance.

Third, they look like something out of a nightmare. Long, draping fabric over brittle bodies. Like the Ghost of Christmas Yet to Come. I never get the chance to see their faces. Some have hoods too heavy and others have veils pulled tight over their features. Those are the worst. It's as if they're pushing through some kind of barrier. Literally stretching and straining the veil, if you believe in that sort of thing. I used to. Ted has never been one for scary stories. Scientifically minded, he had always come up with the answers to how magic tricks were done, how psychics "knew" things, how the water glass moved itself off the counter. I could really use him to see the things and tell me it was all ok, that it really was just a trick of the light, just a cataract forming in my eye, just an undocumented side effect of my meds. But he was too afraid to try. To even admit they could be anything but my "overactive imagination". It isn't my imagination. I know it isn't. But at the same time, I don't know if I can believe in something like monsters either.

I don't know why it is so much harder to believe when I have proof. But it isn't proof, I suppose. Seeing isn't always believing. Not until someone else could confirm what I'm seeing. Not until I know that I'm not the only one.

By Monday, I drag my sleepless, and certainly smelly by now but definitely hungry, self to the store down the street. The soccer moms doing their pre-pick-up-the-kids shopping keep giving me strange looks. At first I think it must be my messy hair and sweatpants, but I don't give them much attention after I realize that I'm outside, out of my house, more than a mile away, and the shadows are still there. The other customers are probably watching me step cautiously around objects they apparently can't see, flinch at every little thing and go out of my way to reach produce from a distance. It isn't my fault that shadows are blocking my path and I feel more fear thinking about touching them than I do just being in their presence. By the time Thursday comes again, I'm ready to tell Dr. Baron everything. I need help, of the funny farm variety. But how do you ask for help without just being sent to the funny farm? I start with "I've gone legitimately insane" today. Apparently, having a hold on my mental standing and recognizing the crazy means I'm perfectly sane, shadow creatures on my tail or not.

"I'm telling you, they just showed up and now they're just *there*. All the time." I shift on the memory foam chair. I picked this one instead of the larger, lonelier couch today. It had looked so comfortable and it wasn't occupied by my own personal fleet of dementor wanna-bes. The problem was, the memory foam remembered too many different bottoms and was currently making mine slide right off the chair in a way that has me holding onto the arms in a vice grip and planting my feet. That, and you know, the dementor fleet.

"Doing what exactly?" Dr. Baron leaned forward in her own chair, probably perfectly and comfortably molded to her ass, blissfully unaware of the shadow looming behind her.

"I don't know. They just stare at me!" I can't help but shout. No one listens, we had just one over this.

"Try to calm down, Liv." I hated that nick-name. It was a childhood nick-name. One *he* had dragged back into my adult life after everyone else had left it in the past where it belonged. It was the name everyone soon adopted in his stead and a name that used to make me smile so easily. Now it's just a name that constantly tells me to do exactly what I want, I want to give up.

"Livia." I say, letting the sorrow weigh down my breath instead of the panic for the first time in days.

"I'm sorry." She wasn't, she said the name on purpose to push a button. Most sessions I am Miss Moss. Today was not the day to be pushing buttons. Maybe I could train the shadows to be my attack dogs. I move my eyes to the one right behind Dr. Baron's armchair. It seems they can't read minds. "Let's go back to the beginning. When did this first start happening?"

"It's complicated."

"How so?"

"Well…" I can say they started a couple weeks ago, but thinking back to the things I have been seeing out of the corner of my eye confuses me. They were one in the same, right? "With… with that night, I think."

"But you're not sure?"

"That was the first night I saw something out of the corner of my eye. But I was a little distracted with the whole situation to pay it much attention. I thought I was just, you know. Paranoid. I'm being followed, someone else did this and they're still out there, corner of your eye stuff."

"But now you don't think so?"

"No." I let out a frustrated sigh. This isn't the detail I want to talk about. I want to know what they are, if anyone else can see them, or if they are completely in my head. I want to nip this thing in the bud. In two days I will be returning to work. Life is already complicated enough without jumping out of my skin every time something that isn't really there moved. I don't even know how I'm going to get out of bed with the crippling fear sending my heart into hummingbird beats. I take a deep breath. "Two weeks ago, I saw something from the corner of my eye and I followed it. Usually the corner of my eye thing would just not be there if I looked but this time it was. It just stood in the hallway like my own shadow and when I blinked it was gone."

"Are you positive that it wasn't your shadow?"

I am pretty sure the look I shoot across at Dr. Elizabeth Baron should have had her bones and skin withering and face melting off like the Nazis in Raiders but the woman just continues to scribble in her folder. "I told myself that at first, but no. It wasn't." And now that I am trying hard to think about it, I don't think that was the first time either. Something, a memory, scratches at my mind until I give it my attention.

*****

I was nine, clutching my shins tight as I buried my scrunched nose into my knees and braced for impact. I didn't care about splashing. It was the summer that I was finally old enough to swim alone. I used to love the water rushing by my ears and the white noise that swam around my head. It was dizzying and chilling in the best way possible. I would let my limbs relax and little bubbles float from my nostrils as I slowly sank to the bottom of the pool until my lungs started to scream and I'd push off the bottom to rocket to the surface. It wasn't a huge pool. Not anymore. The year before I could barely skim the bottom with my toes, but that summer I could almost walk on my knees. I could now stay in the cool blue water to my hearts' content. But at the same time, it wasn't as fun anymore. I noticed the leaves and bugs floating around me more than when I was younger. And it was eerie without my mother reading a book on the pool deck and watching me mimic seals and mermaids with the patience of a saint. I looked into the little wooded area that met our carefully manicured backyard for any signs of people or animals. It felt like I was being watched, and not by the smothering eyes of my mother checking through the window. It felt more like I was being spied on. Or hunted.

I sank back into the water, letting my hair spread around me and blowing out slowly through my nose to just let my eyes stay above the surface as I slowly spun around.

Nothing. No nosy neighbors. No dog walkers. No one.

I rolled my eyes and heaved myself back onto the deck to jump again. I ran from the little gate at the top of the stairs, my feet barely keeping traction against the slick hot metal with little puddles of algae taking over. I launched myself into the cold water and listened to all the little bubbles swimming for the surface. Still clenched in my little ball, I opened my eyes. There was something dark in the water. Like hair. Like someone with really long black hair jumped in after me and it was floating all around us. Something inside me froze at the sight and made me forget where I was as I took in a breath through my nose. My throat burned as I stood and coughed at the surface, hot water leaking out my nose and eyes.

My vision was blurry from the chlorine but I didn't see anything in the water. Still, I rushed in a panic to the side of the pool and pulled myself out.

"Mom!" I yelled around a cough. "Mom!" My mother's head appeared out the sliding screen door on the deck.

"What Livia? I don't have time to play today." "There was someone in the pool." I said, feeling guilty and stupid as I pointed at the empty water rippling in front of me. There was nothing there. No one followed me out, no one pushing past me to escape down the stairs and into the back yard. Still, I felt scared.

23

"Livia. I told you to stop watching that stupid movie. There is nothing in the house and no one in the pool." My mother looked frustrated but still stepped out onto the deck to look around and make sure. "Why don't you come inside? It's almost time for dinner."

"This has nothing to do with Jumanji! There aren't even any pools in it!"

"Inside Liv. Now."

I would usually jump back into the pool once more to smooth out my hair and get all the little leaf bits from the deck off of my skin, but I didn't want to go back in that water right now. I grabbed my towel and didn't even want to wipe off my face, fearing what I wouldn't be able to see. My mother seemed to notice but didn't say much.

"Come on Liv. Inside. Don't forget to put up the stairs." I did as my mother said, lifting the stairs and locking them into place on the gate. I pulled the towel tighter around myself as the evening breeze picked up and followed me up the stairs on the deck and into the house. "Are you positive that it wasn't your shadow?" my mother asked. The question just made me angry, I don't remember why.

*****

I remember that summer. Fourth grade. The summer right after my grandmother died, when my grandfather would come over for dinner and my mom always seemed so much more tired than usual. I don't remember swimming much that year. I even remember my father being upset over how much money he spent opening the pool for no one to use it. I still don't like to swim alone, but I think I now understand why all of a sudden as a kid I hated swimming in lakes or the ocean when I couldn't see my feet. I had never thought about it before now. I remember having a lot of nightmares that year all because of a stupid movie. A lot of hidden enemies in the jungle beyond my back yard or being swept into a board game to wait in the dark for years and years. Why was this pool dream any different? I ignore the little part of myself telling me that it was never

24

a dream. Because it had to be. These things couldn't possibly have been in my life for so long without me noticing.

Dr. Baron looks at me for a long moment before writing something in her quick, scratchy script.

I decide to tell her everything, the nightmares, the waking up to things staring at me from my own bed, and of the days that followed. I talk about how I would have a panic attack when anything was closed around me and I couldn't see what was behind it like the shower curtain or my closet door. But at the same time, how I can't sleep with the bedroom door open. As if keeping it closed kept them out, which I knew was in no way true. Or maybe it's because I couldn't see what was in the darkness of the hallway and I am convinced eyes that I can't see were on me. I tell her that I now have another reason I can't function besides the crippling depression, and that my anxiety is through the roof and no, I haven't been taking my medication because they make me feel even worse somehow and I need to be completely clear headed.

The little ding of Dr. Baron's timer goes off and rings through my next thought. It looks like I wouldn't get to have my suicide ideation and talk down this week. I probably wouldn't have had the nerve to bring it up anyway.

Dr. Baron organizes her folders and walks back to her desk. "Maybe we should go back to weekly appointments, hmm?" She peers over her glasses at me as I stretch out from my awkward seat in the old chair.

I mull it over for a second, it's probably for the best. "Okay." I should really be in here every day.

"Alright. Well, right now I am all booked up, but I will put you in my computer to start weekly again at the beginning of next month." Typical. I roll my eyes at yet another disappointment from this woman. "Now, about these hallucinations. You've already had a scan for your migraines. Nothing is wrong with you physically. I think with you starting back here soon you would like to avoid being admitted for a mental health eval, yes?" She doesn't pause for my answer. I want to do whatever is necessary to end this and if work had to wait, well, it wouldn't be the first time. It would actually be a relief at this point. "In my professional opinion, I think this is fear.

You've been isolating yourself. A social environment like work will do you good. All of your licenses are up to date. Go back to work this time Miss Moss. These stress induced illusions will disappear as soon as you've adjusted. You'll see." The doctor turns her little desk clock towards herself and gets up to put my file away in the large cabinet behind her desk, pulling out the next patients'. "Now I'm running late. If the problem persists you know you can call me right? Anytime Miss Moss and I'll get back to you as soon as I have a moment. Have a good day. Get out. Get some sun." Dr. Baron makes a shooing motion with her hand and I let myself out.

"You know you can always call me right? Anytime Miss Moss." I mimic to myself to the distaste of the secretary clacking away at her computer. It was probably Sharon. Sharon could suck it.

Tell that to the voicemails and messages that you never returned I had wanted to say, I don't know what stopped me. Some ingrained lizard brain part of me knowing not to piss of the only person who could help I guess. I bow my head against making eye contact with anyone else and leave, avoiding the shadow at the door as I did.

I start the walk home to an empty apartment. I'm twenty-eight and still not used to living alone. Ted had lived with me for a while and it was nice... for a bit. When you're alone you always feel like you need someone and when you have someone you always want space. Having my big brother move in was a bit claustrophobic and messy for my taste most days. I had needed time on my own to heal so three months later Ted had moved back in with his girlfriend to give me that healing space. Well, I have been alone for just over two months now, and instead of healing, my wounds have festered to the point where they were leaking hallucinations and paranoia into my life. I'm living a nightmare, and no one seems to notice or care because I have cut out or pushed away everyone who could have been here to help.

Maybe that's why the shadows chose me, because I'm so lonely. Or maybe they chose me because I'm alone.

Easy prey.

It's a terrifying thought to have just as I slide my key into the deadbolt on my apartment door. Welcome home.

CHAPTER FIVE

I need to regulate my sleeping schedule a bit. In two days I'm going back to work after a long break. Last March it was just supposed to be two weeks, returning by April 6th. Two weeks turned into a "I'm just not ready to be back here" meltdown on my first day which got me a third week and a psychiatrist.

During the fourth week, there was kind of this mutual *'it's been a month, come back or you're fired / I can't deal with this right now, I quit.'* That led to a summer of friends constantly inviting me to rides out to the beach, Ted going on weekend trips with his love and various other happy suntanned people that I didn't have the time for. Well, all I really had was time, but I needed to keep a close watch of my savings if I wasn't ready for a job. It was as good of an excuse as any other. And the last thing I needed to get me ready was so many happy, sun kissed people gloating about vacations, adventures, and lovers. It's when I started staying inside. And inside led to in my room. Which led to bed.

It's lucky that I managed to keep a few understanding work friends who left my personal life alone when I wasn't there to gossip with them but still gave me little updates about what was going on at the hospital and which jobs were available to apply for. Some people just didn't know how to be pushed away. It probably helped that a nurses' schedule doesn't amount to much free time to notice when you were being pushed away. Another bit of luck had the months after my firing/quitting filled with people hired and fired quickly for not being able to handle the simple task of checking vitals without attempting to steal pain killers or personal effects and three cases of maternity leave.

I reapplied for my old position in July and was rehired to a different department. At the time I was given a two month prep period before the other RN left for her maternity leave. This would normally be used for training, but in this case with me returning to the same hospital within the same year, the two months were filled with mandatory psychiatric evaluations with Dr. Baron. Now, Tiffany was leaving for her maternity leave and I am due to come in and fill the position until either Tiffany returns or I am hired on permanently. My bank account and I were hoping for the latter before the two weeks from hell.

Now I just don't have the energy. I have to keep telling myself that time is up. I need to go back. And this is it, if I bail on the hospital again they will never hire me back. It's frankly a surprise they did this time.

I mostly slept through August and then started hallucinating during the first week of September, had a big freak out, and now only two days were left before I had to figure out how to completely switch my manic sleeping schedule and not flip out while refilling water and ginger ale pitchers. This was going to be fantastic.

Two days, a dozen more melt downs, some ZQuil and seven alarm settings added to my phone later and the smell of John Adams Hospital hit me just as badly as the last time I had tried to come back. I have to push myself into the elevator and up to the third floor nurses station where I needed to check in. Tears stung and threatened to fall but hell no, crying was for home alone in bed, not public places and definitely not at a job that was only mine until the other shoe fell. The dreaded emergency room was an entire street away. Another building. Only connected by a sky bridge on a different floor. This was practically a completely new work place. No need for flash backs or panic attacks.

"Liv, you're alive!" Courtney runs up to me in mismatched scrubs-Care Bears on top and dinosaurs on the bottom.

"Yeah. First day back. How are you?" I try not to look at the shadow studying my bubbly coworker, seemingly perplexed by her attire. But it can't be perplexed. Perplexed would mean… I don't exactly know but it was too human for my comfort level and the anxiety issuing from the thought has me wanting to scream and run away.

"Nothing much. Still working with the kiddies I but wanted to come up and see you. That and avoiding Sekina, and here she comes. Sorry, not sorry, catch ya later!" Courtney grabs an armful of paperwork over the nurse's station and waggles her eyebrows before practically bolting back to the children's unit. Sekina was going to be my new manager? Great. Hopefully she would at least remember who had trained her while she was still in nursing school and working as an aide. Most of all I just want Sekina to let me have full hour lunches on Thursdays so I could keep my current appointment slots with Dr. Baron, but there was slim chance of that happening. I'd be lucky if I got a scheduled lunch at all.

As the scowl faced woman waddles towards me and the shadow disappears around the corner after Courtney, I have to stop and think about why I am here again. Why I had even gotten into nursing in the first place. I like people enough, but it was just so draining both physically and emotionally. It's a job where no one ever thanked you for your long hours with anything other than aiming some vomit on your scrubs instead of your socks. I could have been anything. I could have used my people skills and endless patience on a desk job with a hefty pay like Nick had or been a starving artist like Ted or a computer programmer like Ted's girlfriend. An astronaut, a teacher, an actress… a writer. Why am I here? And then I take a deep breath and accept that yes, I could have been absolutely anything I wanted, but for some crazy reason I had chosen nursing and most of the time I loved this job.

It's nice to be back, if not a little nerve wracking what with possible psychosis simmering under the surface. I had started out in Post-Op when I was fresh out of college, it was always busy and full of medication requests and fussing family members, people who wanted to go home, people who wouldn't listen to anyone but their doctor (even though the residents and nurses did the brunt of the work). It had been general insanity in the form of healing. My time in the Emergency Room was more to my pace, always something to do, new things to learn, and plenty of writing material people had joked. But my time there had been short and something I don't think about often and wouldn't think about at all today if I could help it.

Now I'm back and I've been moved up to the Intensive Care Unit. Literally up, as in top floor, not a higher position. Who would get a higher position after all the trouble I had put my bosses through before leaving? No. The ICU isn't exactly a demotion, but it is a job people either choose as a passion or are forced into.

It isn't necessarily a bad place to be put but it's quiet and, well, depressing. Everyone on the floor is either dying, unconscious, or in extreme pain and most who were awake barely said a word. The feeling of death seems to always hover right behind you and follow you into rooms and stair wells until you could finally escape the hospital all together. I don't need more things following me right now. I have enough darkness on my tail, but I can't say no to the pay or the insurance and it isn't the worst place I could be.

I'm snatched out of my introverted analysis of the situation by Sekina slapping down a pile of charts on the countertop next to me.

"So, I'm your Charge Nurse for this unit now, Kayla is still the Head for the floor. That means you're going to be listening to what we say and not doing whatever the hell you want." Sekina says while eying me up and down with a brow raised like she could see the crazy wafting off of me. Maybe she could. "Now, technically you are a new hire so you're supposed to go through the training and shadowing, but the last of the warm weather is making people do the crazy shit they do and we are full up and understaffed. You have been here over four years regardless of a little… break" She pauses to eye me again. Sekina's emphasis of the word leaves no confusion as to her meaning. She thinks I'm crazy. Broken. I must pass some kind of visual evaluation or maybe Sekina is just trying to see how I will react to the word because either way, she continues. "So, basically, I'm not going to waste my time. Why don't we both sign this pretty paper here next week and say we did it, huh?" As Sekina slides the training evaluation form with its carbon copy into an inbox in front of her computer, one of my shadowy friends reappears behind her, seeming to read it over. I silently pat myself on the back for not jumping. "So just don't fuck up." I hear as I watch the shadow reach out and touch Sekina's lilac scrubs. I feel my eyes widen and I gulp down too much air while Sekina just looks on like there isn't a giant reaper-thing playing with her sleeve. There probably isn't. The shadow looks back to me and I avert my eyes. "Liv?" Crap, I probably have that *just saw a ghost* stare going on. "You okay?"

"Yeah, fine." No I'm not, I am pretty sure that I'll never be fine again. But I have to try.

"Alright. I have some scheduling to figure out and other paperwork to file. I'm going to split my charts in half because I think you are more than capable of handling all of them on your own, but I want to start you off slow and as I said, I am busy. Sound alright with you?"

"Yeah. Do my best."

And I do.

I'm told I will only be allowed four patients under my care because they want the nurses to keep a calm and critical eye on their patients at all times. In post-op I would have had up to ten, sometimes more if there were a lot of emergency surgeries that day. A part of me misses the noise and adrenaline of rushing around the busier floor, but another little piece of me screams at a different kind of nervous energy associated with the emergency and post-op wing. It was a different part of my life, and I know I never want to see that building again. Just passing the sky bridge connecting them makes me nauseous. Maybe working in ICU would give me a better outlook on life. Maybe it will make me want to live every day I have because you never know when your last will sneak up on you.

I doubt it.

I've been through a lot of experiences that I was supposed to turn a positive view on and have yet to find any bright spots in the dark.

Every round I go back and give Sekina a status on each of her patients to the point where the RN is getting aggravated by the near constant interruptions. I check machines, make sure blankets are tucked in and that everyone is as comfortable as they can be. I make sure the warming cabinets are full should any one need a warm blanket and that everything is fully stocked. I never stop walking back and forth between rooms no matter how exhausted I become and how tempting the chair by Sekina is. There are just two hours left to my shift when a young man is brought up. He doesn't belong to anyone yet and Sekina gives me the chart. My first patient. All mine. Not shared or pawned off so someone else could fill in time sheets. The patient's name is Samuel James Marsh. Assault and battery, patient in coma, just had surgery for a punctured lung, brain damage, and internal bleeding. On a respirator. Drug abuse indicated, amphetamines present in blood work. There is no insurance and next of kin is a brother, Noah, no power of attorney yet. No DNR. I hear the brother before I see him running into the unit calling the patient's name only to be waylaid by Sekina and lectured about his surroundings and the need for quiet.

I follow the gurney in, adjusting the blankets and checking that the IV is set up properly and that the ventilator is an appropriate distance from the bed. I see the brother trying to fight his way into the room around the orderlies as Dr. Carson attempts to explain the situation. I pull an under stuffed, pea soup green chair to the side of the bed without the machines for the brother to use once he calms down. I would want one if something had happened to Ted. I place the chart at the foot of Mr. Marsh's bed and turn around to greet the brother as he listens intently to the doctor, but I'm met by a shadow standing by the ventilator and leaning into the face of the patient. I freeze. The brother doesn't take that as a good sign and starts shouting questions again, demanding to know what is wrong.

"Nothing, it's fine. She's just checking the machines are functioning properly. Right Liv?"

I nod my head and force my numb lips into a smile I hoped is convincing but feels awful shaky. "They're fine." I repeat the doctor's words and move out of the room with the shadow, feeling guilty about leaving it so close to someone who can't defend himself. But what am I supposed to do? And this one was different, I think to myself, it is huge and it isn't looking at me, just this Samuel Marsh. Maybe the patient used to be able to see them too. The thought has me nearly ready to faint again.

"Welcome back Livia, we missed you." Dr. Carson says softly with a smile on his way out of the room. I recognize his bedside manner sneaking into his usual dry delivery. "Try to keep it together this time, okay?" He winks playfully and shuffles off, flipping through another chart as I try to cool the heat on my face with my freezing fingers. That wasn't embarrassing at all. Nice to know people still remember me. I only wish it had been for my work ethic.

And so goes my week. I take on any new patients that enter the unit, slowly giving Sekina back her own, and am handling the situation as best I can. Everything goes far better than I expected, the constant activity being a wonderful distraction from crazy life. I have a moment of pride in my accomplishment of a nearly full work week without any issues as I head to my chair behind the nurses station to check over a few things and sit for a while. It isn't long before my proud bubble pops.

From the nurse's station, I watch the big shadow pace by my patient's bed. It gets up close to the ever watchful brother and rages, shakes, looks like it's trying to scream but nothing ever happens. It hovers over the patient again before going back to pacing. What did it want? Was it waiting for the patient to die? Is it mad because the surgeons saved him?

Maybe they were reapers. They must be. They were everywhere and I could see them because I was supposed to be dead. Oh God, I think, did that mean my time really was up? Were they waiting around me like this one was waiting for the patient to crash again?

My stomach drops and I stand there as if I am about to play the hero and vanquish these beasties back to their realm. But then the raging shadow stops where it is getting close to the brother again and looks up. If it had eyes, they would be boring right into mine. I can't move, can't blink. It's like seeing them for the first time all over again. All that fear chokes my heart as the blood drains from my face. The thing moves and my eyes track it. I don't mean to, don't want to. I still have trouble looking directly at them without pulling a cowardly lion right out the nearest window, but now it is as if the fear has glued my eyes to the shadow. The Reaper. It moves again and so do my stupid eyes and then it stands up to its full, very intimidating height. This was definitely the biggest one. Shit. And then it moves towards the door and leaves the room. *Shit.*

The shadow moves right to me as my knees finally give out and I fall back into the chair. I can feel my eyes widening the closer it gets until it is right in front of the station and I am looking up at the form towering over me. This was bad. What do I do? All I can think is a mantra of no no no no no! I let that take over. "No." I whisper in a voice soft, but firm. It doesn't seem to hear or care so I bring up the volume, just a little, as much as I can manage. "No." It lets out a huff of air that feels like electricity dancing over my skin and I use all of my courage to close my eyes as I think, *this is it, good-bye cruel world.*

And then, nothing. I open my eyes and the reaper thing has already moved back into Marsh's room, pacing again. It had listened. I don't know why that seems to pull another chord of terror in me. Is it listening in an animalistic, territorial, you are standing your ground, I'm going to back off to my territory way? Or did it understand what 'no' meant? And if it did, what else did it understand?

Every once in a while it looks at me. Sometimes it will follow me out of the room after checking on the brothers, but now I know, at least one of them will listen.

The day is almost over when all hell breaks loose. The shadow starts to fidget, darting in and out of my line of sight. It's making me more uncomfortable than usual as I'm trying to concentrate on my end of shift paper work. I get up to do one more round, to get away from the disconcerting distraction, but the thing chases after me, caging me into the station. I'm about to panic when the alarm goes off. "No no no no no not now." I say when I see what room it's coming from. The shadow zaps back into Marsh's room, reaching the bedside just before me.

"What's happening? These machines are supposed to keep him alive why the fuck aren't they working?" The brother screams at me from his station by Sam's side. He is nearly cutting off the circulation to his hand with the tight grip he was wringing it with.

"Mr. Marsh, I need you to stay calm while I work, I'm going to fix this okay. Just stay back!" I take the pillows out from under Sam's head, make sure his airways are clear, that the tube was still secure and functioning. His lungs shouldn't be tiring this quickly. Dr. Carson rushes into the room taking over, barking orders at me to get the brother out as Sekina dashes in with the crash cart. "Noah, please come with me, we're going to pull him through this, okay? Please, give the doctor space." Noah backs out of the room, hands in his hair, frantically peering around me. He won't let me close the door, wedges his torso between me and the door frame.

We listen to round after round as minutes pass and the alarm still sounds. I am certain that this is it, that Sam's body is too tired and abused to continue on. From the look on Noah's face, he knows what it means too, but that look quickly turns to anger as he brushes past and demands we try again. "One more time! Just one more! Please!"

I'm not sure if it's a blessing or prolonged torture when they get the patient stabilized again. The answer becomes clear when the doctor pulls the chart and his face twists, eyes pinning me to the spot.

"With me Moss. Now."

Noah looks confused. "I'll be right back." I tell him calmly as Sekina tends to the patient.

"Don't make promises you can't keep." Dr. Carson hollers back, marching to the nurse's station and slamming my patient's chart down. I wait while he rubs his eyes. "Where do we keep the DNR patient's names, Moss?"

"I—"

"Right here. We keep them in the first line on the chart, and we keep them next to the code alarm board. Do you know why?" He doesn't give me a second to process the question let alone answer before he's speaking again. "So that when the patient codes you can see if you have to go through the trouble of paging me or not. Can you tell me why I was paged for this patient?"

I reach for the chart, I'm sure I had filled out all the proper paperwork for Sam. He was my first, my only patient at the time. My complete responsibility. I look through the paperwork Noah had filled out while his brother was in surgery, there was nothing about a DNR. But as I flip through I find a copy of Sam's license. Organ Donor. DNR. *Crap.*

"The brother—"

"I don't care what his brother filled out. The patient's license clearly states his wishes. Fix it. And inform the idiot brother that this won't be happening again unless he goes to court and becomes the POA. Are we clear?"

I nod, "Yes Dr. Carson. I'm Sorry."

"I don't care, go tend to your patient. Sekina!" He speaks loud and firm, but not in the viscous shouting tone I was just subjected to.

I trades places with the charge nurse, replacing the pillows under Sam's head. Noah is still hovering, holding his brother's hand. "Mr. Marsh, there seems to be a problem with your brother's paperwork."

To say Noah is angry wouldn't even touch the emotion he is currently expressing in the form of red-face yelling he's doing in my personal space right now. I can't get a word in. Sekina watches from the doorway shaking her head, not even trying to help or do her job as head nurse for the unit by taking over the explanation. When he finally tires of shouting and I can explain the Power of Attorney process, Sekina speaks up. Of course.

"What did I tell you this morning?" I can't believe I'm about to be lectured in front of a patient's family for the second time in less than ten minutes. I would have never done this to Sekina.

"I'm doing my best."

"Well do the best of someone better. Clock out Liv. You're done for the night."

I swallow the embarrassment with a deep breath before turning back to Noah. "If it were up to me, I would consider you power of attorney as you're next of kin and your brother is currently brain dead. However, rules are rules. If you do not have the proper paperwork giving you rights to change Sam's living will status, we will not be able to resuscitate him again." Noah won't look at me, he just stands over his little brother shaking his head at the politics. I don't blame him one bit. "Goodnight Mr. Marsh. If you like, I can help you with the paperwork process in the morning." Noah doesn't say anything, but he does grace me with a nod and a sniff in my general direction before I leave.

I am almost out the door and into the quiet of the night when Courtney runs up to me.

"Hey, heard you had a rough day." Sekina always was a rapid gossip. "Wanna go down to Josie's? First rounds on me! Think of it as a welcome back to hell present." She chuckles. Courtney loves her job, but she knows it has always been just a job to me.

"Not tonight. Long day. Thank you though. Maybe... maybe some other time."

I don't think that will ever happen. Too many bad memories associated with Courtney and venting with alcohol. From the look on Courtney's face, she is beginning to know it too.

CHAPTER SIX

March 23, six months earlier

I slam my shot glass down onto the bar as the still scrubbed up nurse beside me laughs and I shake my head around the bitter heat of the bourbon. "He's just been so crazy lately Court! Almost mean." I cough out.

"You're the one that offered your not so shiny paycheck for the very much shiny apartment when your bro left him hanging to move in with whatsherface. You got yourself into this mess."

"Thanks. So supportive." I do my best to deadpan, flagging down the bartender for refills. "But seriously. He wasn't like this when Ted lived there. He was just this shy, rich dude that helped me change my major to one that would actually get me a living wage and he'd bring me chocolate milkshakes when finals had me ready to jump off the nearest bridge. We were great friends."

"And he's hot like burning."

"Yeah. There's definitely that." I roll my eyes in a judging glance Courtney's way. It wasn't untrue, but I was trying not to objectify here.

"Hey." Courtney pointed, leaning a little heavily on the bar. "You never said you had another major. What, were you like one of those hippie philosophy girls? I could see that. Do you have a good brownie recipe? I could go for some brownies right about now."

"Thanks, but no. English actually. I wanted to be a writer."

"Well, the hospital must be giving you plenty of material."

"That's what I said! I was just talking about getting back into it. But noo. I should go back to school, get another degree. Blah blah blah! For what? To clean up more puke, blood and shit? Please. I'm miserable enough already."

"Such an angry drunk you are." Courtney points at me around her shot glass with a pout. "If you hate it so much then quit." She shrugs, throwing back her refill and grabbing the bartender's sleeve to shove the glass at him. She watches the bartender fill it to the brim before picking it up and swirling it around, pinky in the air. "Be one of those scholarly folk. Write a novella and retire to the country to work on your memoirs or whatever that *50 Shades of Grey* bitch did. Retire me while you're at it, please."

I feel my face scrunch up and groan. I have made my feelings about that particular book series very clear to Courtney on past bar trips. So much money for twilight fanfiction and banking on the misunderstanding of the BDSM community. But that wasn't the point right now. Courtney probably brought it up on purpose. The nurse knows how easy it is to goad me into a ramble, she had been on the receiving end of enough of them in the break room. "I don't think that's how it works. Besides, it wouldn't be very *responsible.*"

"Who's the dream crushing asshole you're quoting?"

"Who do you think?"

Courtney sips at her shot, putting on her thinking face before yelling, "Nick!"

"Ding ding ding!" I bounce a little dance in my seat, waving my hand I'm like a ringing bell.

"Haha! Go me! So that's why you're a nurse? To be responsible?" Courtney is definitely judging me now, giving me the same look she gave the idiot teenager this morning who broke both of his arms and his collarbone riding a grocery cart through the Prudential Center parking garage.

"Yup."

"That's not a good reason."

I huff out a laugh. "Oh yeah? What's yours?"

Courtney shrugs again, twirling her glass through some spilled something or other. "I like people. Like making them feel better."

"Yeah, because that's what we do."

"It is!"

"Then why did I see three people die today, have two families break down on me and get yelled at by a million others about their pain or my personal favorite, their doctors and their food?"

"You really are miserable."

"I'm just being a realist."

"Hmm." Courtney hums thoughtfully, continuing to spin her glass while giving me the side eye.

"What?"

"That's a funny way of pronouncing pessimist." She grins. "Come on Liv. Death doesn't affect you, just the people around you. I'm pretty sure you know that. We all learn that day one if not sooner. Now, enough about work if it pisses you off so much. Tell me more about the hottie and how horrible it is to be in a loving relationship with a well off, beautiful man. I need to live vicariously through somebody." She giggles, a little past tipsy.

"There's not much to tell because we're not in a relationship! We're friends. At least that's what I thought we were. Best *friends*. I didn't realize moving in together was *moving in together*." I air quote. "I love him. He loves me, a little more than I love him. We drive each other insane."

"Bow chica wow wow!"

"Not even close. Like nuts. Crazy. A view of four padded, white walls instead of silk sheets and sunsets." I lean forward and rest my arms against the bar. I miss him, he had always been a little overbearing but in a cute, worried mother hen way. Now it was bordering on abusive and controlling and I don't know how to handle that. I don't understand where it's coming from at all. How do I even begin to figure it out? "I miss the him he was when Ted was around. This Nick walks into the bathroom while I'm in the shower to use the toilet. And I'm not talking about just to pee. This Nick is always telling me to *be more!* in a way that isn't even at all supportive of the job I already have and that he convinced me to take to begin with! His expectations are so friggin' high, he's chronically disappointed in me and it hurts. I don't know how to deal with that. It's like he's making me his pet project or trophy wife in training or something. And! *We're not even actually dating!* Like, what does he friggin' want?" I yell, luckily not quite loud enough in the busy bar to draw too much attention.

"Okay," Courtney wobbles on her stool, grabbing my shoulder and pointing a wavering finger so close to my nose I go a little cross eyed. "What do *you* want?"

It's a question I haven't asked myself in a really long time. It takes me a while to figure out. "To see him happy again. To BE happy, myself." I say because it's what I think I should. I don't know what else to say or where to begin in figuring out a more accurate answer. And who doesn't want happiness? Who doesn't want their friends to be happy? Nick definitely wasn't happy right now.

"Maybe those things don't go together?" Courtney looks guilty for even saying it, resting her head on the side of the bar and pouting up at me.

I take a deep breath and throw back my shot. "I love him, he's a great guy. I don't know, maybe I should give it a shot? Maybe if he felt more secure things would go back to what they were?" I shake my head. Do I really want that? Was it ok to try? What happens if I'm right and later I just want to be friends again? Will it all be ruined? Will we be right back here, alone and complaining to others? "I'm just having a bad day."

Courtney smirks, popping up again. "Then go home, grab the hottie and have a *Good. Night.*"

I roll my eyes but return the smirk, grabbing my purse. I don't think so, more confusing emotions are the last thing we need. "Maybe I will." I teased anyway. Like she said, Courtney has to live through somebody. I wink and hop off the stool.

*****

I'm exhausted. Memories of my last bar crawl with Courtney dance through my mind as I scrub the carpet raw. The coffee stain won't come out. It has never come out any other day I've tried and would most likely never come out.

Not with the carpet scrub or the YouTube tutorials or the landlord's shop vac. It was the strongest coffee in the world, *black as my heart* Nick used to say. It has sat too long. And it wasn't going to come out. Some things can't be fixed.

I slap the half shredded sponge into the bucket of water, dish soap, and vinegar feeling hopeless. All I have accomplished is making the apartment smell like pickled lemons.

I run my pruned fingers through my hair. I could really use a drink. Maybe Courtney was right, maybe I should have gone. I look at the clock. Eleven forty five. It's too late now. I'm exhausted and have work again tomorrow.

I blot paper towels over the damp mess, lightened at best, but probably just spread wider.

I tried.

CHAPTER SEVEN

There's an earth shattering BANG and suddenly I'm waking up in a cave. My heart drops and I barely have time to think or register that I'm hurt before wind is whipping sand into my face and the scene changes before my eyes.

It's loud. Indescribable. Nothing I've ever heard in a theater or on the Fourth of July or anywhere else.

Bangs.

Flashes.

Screaming in the wind.

I crawl as fast as I can, as far as I can reach, and dig into the sand and glassy edges of things I can't see without the flashing over my head and in the sky. The thick, heavy fabric on my stomach bunches and pulls over sharp rocks, grinding sand into my skin. The pain in my leg makes spots dance in front of my eyes.

But then I see him. Shawn.

No.

Something rips through me. A bullet, a scream, I don't know anymore, can't tell. All I know is pain and fear.

Failure and guilt.

I cover Shawn's soaked and gasping body with my own. I made a promise. I close my eyes and do something I swore I would never do over here. I pray.

I know I'm in a plane. A loud one. A box the size of Shawn is next to me.

I know Doctors and nurses are rushing around. There's less pain than I deserve. Calm colored walls. There's a hand scratching my scalp and petting down a beard I hadn't realized I'd grown. That soft hand is coaxing me awake. I know Maggie's face—I'd seen every emotion cross those features from preschool to deployment, but not the one she was wearing now. I know I've put that look there, those dark circles and pale lips, that creased brow.

"Manny."
I open my eyes.

*****

I slam air into lungs that feel as if they've been shut down all night while I slept. I sit bolt upright, grasping the sheets under me and ringing them in my hands, proving to myself that they weren't the scratchy, over-bleached, low thread count of hospital ones.

Static races across my fingertips, a familiar feeling that has me looking down. My lungs stop dead in my chest again as my eyes take in the dark shape covering my hand. I whip myself up and out of the bed, not taking my eyes off the figure reclining in my own damn bed.

"No! Absolutely not!"
The phantom doesn't even spare me a glance as it rolls onto its side, looking like it was going back to sleep. *What the literal hell?* Did these things actually sleep? Well, it wasn't going to here.

"I said no. Get out! Right now!" The other shadow, the tall one at the hospital, it listened. Why wouldn't this one? "Go. Move!" It moved alright. The thing reared back and flashed right in front of me with a speed that wasn't possible. Its formless face stretched behind the veil as if it were wailing or screaming but only a high pitched buzzing could be heard, like the little hairs inside my ears were screaming and not this human sized ghoul. It reaches both hands up and shoves them through me. Cold and static race down my spine before the thing lowers itself back down in the spot on the bed I had abandoned and lays there, turning its head to face the opposite wall before disappearing.

I stand there shaking, clutching my shoulders where the thing had touched me. It had pushed me. It had tried to be violent towards me.

I needed a shower. Needed to wet down the static clinging to my arm hair. Need to forget that feeling. Need to forget that even if they can't touch me, I can still feel them trying.

Next to me is that little one again, preening in another beam of sunlight. It looks harmless enough but that is probably its plan. I sink down to the floor and take a deep breath in the tight space between the bed and the wall.

It is going to be one of those days. "Please. Please let me by. I don't think you understand but-." I look up and the shadow is gone. This day could end now. I would give anything to crawl into bed and get some sleep uninterrupted by a horror show, but at the same time I don't think this bed will be calling my name anytime soon. Maybe I would actually take my medicine tonight. Even if they don't do what they were prescribed for, at least the antidepressents guaranteed a dreamless sleep.

The first alarm on my phone starts playing an annoyingly cheerful melody and I reach up to swipe my fingers across the screen until one connects on the right path. Shower. I need a shower and some food.

Maybe I would stop by the café on my way to work. It wasn't exactly on my route, but it wasn't out of my way enough to stop me, either.

I get up on shaky legs and start my day.

*****

I am lucky enough to even have time to take the long way to work and stop by the Grind House before punching in less than eight minutes late which, according to the hospitals punch clock, is perfectly on time.

I was not so lucky when it comes to who greets me at the counter. I was looking forward to just catching a glimpse of the cheerful baker, not having to interact with him.

"Hello gorgeous."

I freeze. That was new. My hair is still wet and scraped back into a messy bun, the fly-aways being the only places that are dry and currently soaring around my head wildly from the wind. I'm pretty sure these were my slightly stained scrubs too, but I don't want to look down and draw attention to them if they are.

"What're you in the mood for?"

And there is that smile. That light at the end of my tunnel. Old Livia might have had the balls to say *you*. Today's Livia was hiding my shaking hands by clutching my wallet.

"Uh, just water?"

"A water?" He looks a little disappointed. Maybe I should have gone with something that wasn't free.

"Water." I managed to mumble again.

His smile cools a little but is still there, something I would keep with me through the day. "We have bottles in the cooler over here," he gestures to the register, bringing a shadow hovering behind the counter to my attention, "or did you want iced?"

"Ice?" I repeat. I feel like a two year old. Why did I do this to myself today? Did I really need anything else in my life to be embarrassed about?

"Ok, anything else?" I was having a hard time seeing the baker's bright light through the shadow that has come to hover next to him. I shake my head, looking down at my wallet. "Ok. Hey, here." I hear the glass door next to him slide open and the crinkling of parchment paper. "Try one of these. On the house. Maybe you'll try something new next time?" He shoots open a paper bag, the sharp noise making me jump, and slides an enormous muffin inside. He folds over the top and passes it to me before jogging off to fetch my water. Was he so energetic about everything? I feel tired just looking at him.

I manage a small smile, my cheeks shivering from the effort and raise both items slightly in a silent thanks. Maybe I would actually get something for lunch today besides lime Jell-O. I could smell the still melty chocolate through the bag and it's divine. I look forward to it.

*****

Noah sits beside his brother's bed with his head bowed. He looks like a man at the end of his rope. No longer is he shouting, fighting or making impossible demands with even more impossible expectations. He knows what is coming and though he may not be ready to accept it, he seems to be tired of fighting it.

He could be praying or trying to reach his brother telepathically or maybe just resting his eyes from the hurtful sight of his little brother on a bed for the dying. I'm not sure, but I know my heart twinges every time I look at him.

Something in me needs to help him. To prevent him from diving off the deep end that I myself had been struggling not to drown in for months.

Grief is hard.

Guilt is worse.

And from what I've heard of the accident, he has nothing to be guilty about. Sometimes that doesn't matter. With family guilt is usually ingrained deep in there.

Beside him the aggressive shadow still looms. A bit more silent in its stance than usual. Not gesturing its arms as if it were yelling itself raw. Just standing dark and tall, hovering over the little brother with ebbing fists clenched.

Noah looks so weak. I wonder when he slept last. When he ate.

"*Damnit,*" I sigh.

I poke my head into the room and clear my throat to get Noah's attention. "Hey, how are we doing?" He doesn't answer, just brings his bagged eyes back to staring blankly at his brother. Yup, I am going to do it. *Double Damnit.* "How do you feel about chocolate muffins?"

CHAPTER EIGHT

There are some buildings that just live and breathe and as a result, they are never quiet. As a nurse, you get used to the hum of the hospital. All the machines, the people, the noises you have no place for but always seem to be there. When you first walk in it's loud, but the longer you stay the more accustomed you are to the noise. By the time you leave, the silence is what's deafening and it gives a whole new, eerie aura to the outside world while walking home at three AM. Right now it's worse because, I am alone in the dark, walking home through the city at the wee hours of the morning before the birds even bother to chirp. With everything so quiet just crunching a leaf sends my heart into double time. But today there *is* a noise.

I don't notice it at first. It's just another hospital noise. I'm tired and halfway home before the sudden realization of *I'm not in the hospital any more* has me stopping in my tracks to analyze the sound.

As I pause my walk, it gets closer and I find myself sprinting to the closest light post to stand under and search the darkness. I can see nothing but the darkened street, moonlight bouncing off parked car windows, smoggy starlight throwing shadows off buildings, but the noise still follows.

It's a hollow dragging and clicking in long beats until it is right by my side. The hair on the back of my neck prickles and I turn to see the tall shadow step into the halo from a street light.

I press my back against the pole behind me, heart leaping into my throat. My hand moves on its own to fumble the phone from my pocket. It's ringing in my ear before I even realize who I had called.

"Livi, what is it honey? It's late." My mom's voice soothes me. Sometimes you just needed your parents, even if they were miles away and could be of no help at all. Sometimes fear just makes you a child again, crawling into mommy's side of the bed to hide from the monsters under yours.

I can't tell my mother what is going on. I'm lucky Ted hadn't already blown the whistle on that one. But I can talk about my nightmares. Those my mother would understand, would always be there for, right? I can't admit to wanting to give up, it would break my mother's heart, but I could get some words worth fighting for. At least that's what I thought. I'm almost home when things start to get tense.

"Well if this doctor isn't helping you Livi maybe it's time to move on."

"She is helping mom. *I'm* getting better, there are just things going on right now."

"Dreams honey. They're just bad dreams. Aren't you a little old to still be afraid of nightmares?" My mother sighed, blowing static down the line. "It's that city. I told you what living in a city does to someone. You're not socializing. Do you even know your neighbors?"

"You want me to go talk to my neighbors mom? Seriously?"

"No! No, oh my God, they're probably drug dealers! Don't you dare Livia Ann Moss! That neighborhood, I told you Livi. You can come home whenever you want. There's a nice nursing home just a few miles away, even. They're always hiring."

Ever stop to think why? I want to ask.

CHAPTER NINE

I try to stay asleep, I really do, but it's hard to stay in bed with eyes boring into the back of your skull.

I can feel the spot it's looking at sticking out of the blankets, feel the cold stare press against me like the barrel of a gun. I can't go back to sleep but I can't leave my safe little cave of quilts either. If I don't look, I can't see it. My mind circles around the pros and cons in that idea.

Pro, I think to myself, it could all be a part of my imagination or an echo from a nightmare.

Con, what is it doing that I can't see? And if I look, it would know I am awake and I would see it and it would see me seeing it and isn't that how the climax of a lot of horror movies start?

I swallow hard around a dry mouth and throat and curl in on myself. I hear a rustle, it was moving closer. I close my eyes as tight as I can, letting tears slip out, and try to cover the cold spot on my head without being too obvious. I take a deep breath.

It takes a deep breath. A haunted, hollow, dragging breath that clicks at the start and finish.

Mechanical.

Evil.

Not human.

Not like my quick, shaky gasps.

And if I could hear it breathing then it must be close, right by the bed. Waiting. A silent sob shakes me, moving the blanket further down my head and shoulders.

I open my eyes.

The shadow is standing in the spot, in *that* spot that I never look at. It stands tall above me. I launch myself off the couch and barely make it to the bathroom in time to heave into the toilet. I am scared. Petrified. My mind is swimming with visions of shadows on that particular portion of the wall.

I press myself between the toilet and the wall, not wanting anything to sneak up on me. I wait for my stomach to settle, for the anxiety to subside. I take another minute to listen for the hollow breaths and horrible clicking. A different clicking fills my mind and I'm gagging over the bowl again, sobbing at the images flashing through my mind. There's no way I'm making it into work today.

When I can finally stand, I shuffle back to the couch, slow and cautious, making sure I'm alone and that there are no hidden threats ready to send me into another break down.

I call in to work, feeling horrible about it being so soon after starting. Feeling worse when Kim tells me she's going to be locked in to another shift if I don't show up. But I can't. I can't take care of people in this state. I can't be trusted with someone's life.

I call Ted next, needing to talk to someone who might understand at least a small part of the problem.

"It's five in the morning Liv!" He yells after I try reaching him the second time. The call disconnects and I look up to see the tall shadow entering the room again.

"Why are you doing this?" I say, starting to cry, "I don't understand!" It seems to take in my broken state before launching forward, head snapping back and forth with twitches like a wild animal, snarling at an invader to their territory. Roaring. Shrieking.

If I wasn't so terrified I would find humor in how similar the thing's voice sounds to the booming sound effects Christopher Nolan is so fond of. It isn't so funny outside of a movie screen and bursting my eardrums. But this is my territory. If it wants to be animalistic I could be animalistic right back. I stand and put everything I have into a scream, closing my eyes against the force of it. When I open them, it is gone again. I want to feel proud, but all I can feel is fear that it will pop up again the second I let my guard down.

The couch holds no comfort for me anymore. It really never had. I try to relax into the sagging cushions and dented back with my blanket tucked in tight. I don't let my eyes close but I do let them relax as I remember the good old days and this couch.

When Ted and Nick had first rented the place and I was still in college, I was over frequently. There were a lot of memories on this couch. Of homework and pillow fights and movie nights. Soon movie nights became comfortable enough where it was 'movie and fall asleep next to you' nights then 'fall asleep on top of you', and eventually they progressed to shameless cuddling. What really escalated things was the night Nick drank until he was dead to the world on the couch and Ted had told me to take Nick's bed. Sometime in the night in his drunken state, Nick decided his king sized pillow top mattress with countless-thread sheets was more comfortable than Ted's death trap of a bachelor pad sofa and we woke up together in a confused, tangled mess.

After that, the 'gentleman' in Nick decided that I deserved better than the crater filled disaster of a couch that quote – "tried to shank him in his sleep with a busted spring" he had shouted at Ted while recounting his drunken wrestle with the beast over breakfast.

"I swear! It nearly got my spleen! We can afford a new one, why do we have to keep this thing?"

Ted just held in his laughter and hugged his splitting sides as he stood his ground, keeping an extra close eye on us that breakfast to see if we were telling the truth about not *sleeping* sleeping together. "No. That's my couch, I found it and we're keeping it. Respect the couch and it will respect you." He said with narrowed eyes.

"Doesn't change the fact that it smells like the gutter you probably found it in"

"That's not respecting the couch!" Any future sleepovers before I moved in officially, I was invited to share Nick's bed, "With the door open and for Christ sake Liv, wear pants!" being my brother's only rules, though I'm sure Nick got a much harsher list when I wasn't around.

Those nights had been fine. We would turn down the lights, maybe a little small talk about the movie or work in the morning and then we'd fall asleep on our respectful sides of the mattress. In the morning, if we woke up cuddling or practically on top of each other, neither of us said a thing. "We can afford a new one you know," Nick had said untangling himself and moving away from me one morning right before Ted moved in with his girlfriend officially. "If this makes you uncomfortable."

I should have said yes.

I get off the creaking thing and creep down the hall to see if the invaders have left my bedroom and am relieved to see it empty of shadows. I crawl onto the bed, pull the covers around me and sit, tucking myself into one corner to stare out at the room.

I'm not aware of how much time passes before my phone is ringing. I let out a tired sigh and crack my stiff neck back and forth when I see one of the hospital's numbers glaring at me brightly from my phone's screen.

"Hello?"

"Liv, I have Mr. Marsh with a question for you." Sekina says, no shortage on attitude. He is probably driving the staff up the wall with demands regarding his brother. It brings a smile to my face.

"Sure Sekina." There is a rustle as the phone is passed over before Noah Marsh's rough voice crackles through.

"Hey, where are you? You said today was your day on. You promised to check in on him. This Kim chick has no idea what she's doing."

I'm sure that's not the case, the other nurse just probably doesn't let him get away with half of what I do. "I was throwing up, had to call out." I not-quite lie.

"Oh." Noah clears his throat. "Well, feel better. Sam misses you." He gruffs. "And Sekina's a bit—" the line cut off before he can finish, but I don't need him to. Poor thing.

I somehow feel safer after the call. My eyes feel heavy, as if they don't feel the need to be pinned open and alert anymore. I try to fight it but one long blink turns into me *waking up to the light blaring through the window.*

I stretch, popping all my joints perfectly before crawling out from between the expensive sheets and fluffy blankets Nick always kicked to the floor during the night but I can't sleep without. I shuffle down the hall into the kitchen and pause to look at something on the floor. The line of the rug touching the kitchen tiles is a funny color. Like someone spilled something and didn't clean it properly.

"Men." I mumble to myself as I turn on the coffee machine. The glass pot is missing. I look around the counter and over at the kitchen table to see where Nick could have left it but it's nowhere in sight. His keys are still on the counter, where is he? A cool shower would have to suffice over caffeine this morning.

A strange sense of Déjà vu washes over me on the way to the bathroom, but I blame the too few hours of sleep.

I pull back the shower curtain and turn the faucet on, letting the spray wash over my arm to test the temperature. Something is clinging to me, absorbing the water and weighing down my arm. I try to shake it off but the feeling over takes me until it's crushing me, the water dripping though the cloth and drowning me. I back away from the spray, clawing at myself but I can't get free. Everything stops when I see something in the mirror.

A massive, dark shape. Like a person wearing a black cloak. There is no face. I gasp and turn trying to find them, the person responsible for this, my heart is ready to explode out of my chest with the adrenalin pumping through my veins—but there is nothing there. I turn back and see the shadow again. It's turning back around too.

Left, left.
Right, right.
I've done this before. I'm sure of it.
I know the answer, it's right there.
The shape moves with me and it seems to click. The shape in the mirror is me.

I reach up to take the veil from my face, to be unrestricted, but when the darkness is free from my eyes Noah is staring back at me.

I gasp awake, heart beating as hard and fast as it was in my dream.

"Shit. Ugh, why today?"

I try to calm down, but I can't get rid of the frantic feeling that I need to help him. I need to help Noah.

I can't let anyone else go through this.

CHAPTER TEN

"**A**nd how do you feel about that?" Dr. Baron drones. "I don't know. Scared, threatened... insane? How would you feel?"

"Let's keep this about you, shall we Miss Moss?" I slump back against the suede couch stained with other people's tears and problems. Dr. Baron didn't seem to mind talking about herself when she could "empathize". This seems to be out of her ball park. But weren't auditory hallucinations out of the average person's ball park? The psychiatrist hums to herself as she organizes the papers in her lap.

I thought you were supposed to bring up your main issues in therapy sessions to deal with anxiety and depression. I brought up the giant reaper-dementor-shadowy things following me around since... well I thought they might be a factor. Swing and a miss! Maybe I am just crazy.

"Livia?" I nod again, looks like opening up time is over. I let the sarcasm reign until I can go home and crawl back into bed. "Why don't you tell me again what they look like?" Fact checking, typical. Dr. Baron probably has so many patients she couldn't even be bothered to remember my name without my chart, let alone my problems.

"Shadows."

"What kind? Dark and solid? Opaque? Are they just in the corner of your eye?"

"Corner of my eye, right in front of my face, sitting on the other end of this couch." I gesture to the ever present darkness in my life engulfing the opposite corner of the couch, its cloak ebbing tendrils of shadow just within reach of me. I couldn't move any further away, I had tried. "They're everywhere. And dark. Solid. The only part that's lighter or see-through or more shadow like or whatever is what they're draped in. When they move, you can see it."

"Alright. Do they look familiar at all?"

"I can't see their faces and no, I don't know anyone method acting for the role of 'Death' at the moment."

"Well other things can look familiar. Height, the way they move. It's possible you could be projecting the image of someone you know. Someone who may have scared you or that you miss. What do you think?" The thought stings.

"It's not him" I look down and try to smooth over a broken nail with my thumb. "It would be easier if it were."

"And why do you think that?"

"Because then the crazy wouldn't be as scary. I wouldn't be afraid of Nick." Dr. Baron was looking up from her folder again, studying. I hated that look. That's why I haven't been trying to talk about the shadows with anyone since Ted. I don't want to be studied, I just want a solution. "I don't know. They all look different and have different personalities. One in particular is just…" I cringe just thinking about it.

"What, Livia?" I look to my left on the couch at the mass of darkness perched on the arm, glaring without eyes in my direction. Its large chest heaves in mechanical breaths. This is the most still I have ever seen the thing, as if it were pleased I'm talking about it.

"Animalistic, I guess you could say. Large, territorial, loud. Your average asshole." I don't want to admit to it in front of the thing, but a part of me knows it must sense what I'm feeling. "This one scares me the most."

Dr. Baron hums to herself again. "Have you thought anymore regarding the medication we talked about last time?"

I have never liked medication. The ones I've been prescribed for my depression make me feel even heavier but with an added energy that only feeds my anxiety. The prescription usually goes unfilled on my night stand. The anxiety medication makes me feel high and not in control. I need control right now. It is probably okay to be on edge with monsters in your closet. That pill bottle is abandoned with the other. I have just started to feel like myself again, a scared, alone self with super-natural stalkers sure, but myself with no headaches or nausea or missing time. I don't want to do this.

"What you see is real because you see it. I'm not trying to tell you that you have no choice in the matter and that you need this medication right now. But if you take it and they go away, we'll know how to fight them, won't we?" The hulking shadow next to me moves to stand in front of the shrink who is smiling like she's the most brilliant woman in the world. Oh yeah, my patient was hallucinating, I convinced her to take an anti-hallucinogen, aren't I clever? It puffs up, blocking my view and lets out the clicking high pitched shriek it has learned I'm ever so fond of. I can't help the bullet train speed of my heart as I feel like I may faint from fear. That roar from something that couldn't be there in front of the person who was sup-posed to help and instead was having no reaction as if it hadn't been loud enough to crack the windows and shake the Ansell Adams photography off the walls was what did it. It is what typically has me a sobbing mess in bed as it hovers over me or storms about the room. Not today. Dr. Baron looks up, something like confusion or concern on her face. *Did she hear it, feel it? Was it real?* I question. In public I have been able to deal, the people around me ignoring the ever constant flow of shadows made them not as scary, not as real. When I'm alone, that's when they are the most terrifying. No one is there to prove they are all in my head and that I'm in no danger. If Dr. Baron could hear them, "Did you just feel that? Not the right time of day for a train. Do you think it could have been an earth quake?" the psychiatrist asked. *No.* I can't help but think, *they're real. They're really real.*

I have to clear my throat twice before I can look up into the black. "I'll do it. I'll take the medication." It is my last hope, my last chance. If they go away I would be safe, I'd be fine. If they didn't then I am seriously going to need the ghostbusters.

When I get back into the waiting room to walk through the awkward, don't make eye contact with other patients lined up in chairs hallway, I take out my pad and write, Dr. B felt dickwad roar but did not hear at full volume.

I push open the door and hear a noise behind me like the shadow had huffed air through its nose. I don't have to look to know it was reading over my shoulder. "Yeah, that's your name until you earn another one. One day you could even be Rainbow or Daisy. Deal with it." I joke at my could be murderer. Maybe I am crazy. Maybe this prescription would work. I seriously hoped this really had been figments of my imagination. Ted would at least share the victory with me, having called it weeks ago. As suddenly as the shadows arrive, this one is gone. "Well, that is certainly a step in the right direction." Maybe I should name all of them. I snort, yeah, that isn't a whole new level to the crazy or anything.

CHAPTER ELEVEN

I storm past Sekina, who is giving me a judging eyebrow from the nurses' station, and into the Marsh brothers (really Sam's, but hadn't Noah pretty much moved in at this point?) room. "You." I point right at a startled Noah. "You're coming with me." He bristles at the order but I put my fists on my hips, not backing down. Not even with Noah's own personal rage monster in the form of a shadow bulking up and emitting a low growl behind him. "Now. You need food, fresh air and a shower. Your brother isn't going to wake from the sheer force of your stink. Let's go."

Noah almost looks embarrassed, the wind leaving his sails as he glances back at his brother's machines for any sign of change before following me out the door.

I show him to my apartment, let him have a shower and give him some clothes Ted had left behind when he moved out. I offer to wash what he had on but he refuses. I am well aware of how unprofessional the situation is, but I need to do something for him. My dreams are haunting me, I have ghouls haunting me, guilt haunting me. I am done being haunted! I haven't been able to find a way to help myself yet, the new medication doing nothing for me other than heart burn, but maybe if I get this idiot to pull his head out of his ass I could at least save him. The news on his brother hasn't been great. Sam's body was getting used to the medications. His last scans showed his brain is starting to swell again. Slowly, but still a noticeable difference. That combined with the foam developing around his breathing tube was not a good sign. The likelihood of him coming out of this one was small. But miracles could happen I suppose. Either way, I'm not going to let Noah turn into a paranoid hermit like me. He needs to start living again, develop connections, before he has nothing to live for.

When Noah is suitably clean, I drag him over one block west and back towards the hospital, stopping in at the Grind House to try and inspire him out of his funk. I sit him down at a table with a decent enough view of the kitchen and go up to the counter to buy us drinks.

As I wait in line a woman croons, or wails really, over the speakers about broken hearts being blind. Noah argues with me over the bill for a few moments before I pull out my Nurse Ratched voice to get him to back down. As we snack, I attempt small talk. Conversation with him is… difficult. Forced, maybe? Is that the word I'm looking for?

Looking at Noah is like looking into a mirror, but I can't reach through and touch him, just place my hand on the glass and wait for him to place his back. I have a feeling that it's not going to happen tonight, but at least we were out of the hospital and not-alone together.

Baby steps.

As Noah sips at his obnoxiously caffeinated brew with no cream or sugar, I tip my drink slowly back and forth, watching the whipped cream melt and the hot cocoa swirl around and darken the edges of the glossy white inside of the mug. I had picked it on purpose, something sweet and strong smelling, but the rich aroma of the chocolate and happy little sprinkles in my whipped cream was doing nothing to stifle the smell of coffee that had seeped into the walls of the place. As the silence stretches on, I find myself in one of my favorite past times, eavesdropping on the workers and wondering at the source of the laughter from the back where I can't see. Eventually a familiar face bursts through the doors to grab a stack of towels from under the counter. He is animated today, talking loudly about a mess behind the door. A birthday prank gone perfect, apparently.

I turn back to Noah to point it out, but he is just staring into the dregs of his coffee cup like it's his only friend in the world. He doesn't even hear me say his name. He probably isn't ready for something as powerful as that laugh. I feel the smile that I must have caught from the baker slip off my face, leaving my cheek muscles feeling stung and shaky.

I watch him poke at his phone, checking the time or maybe looking for some news. After the third poke I start talking again. I figure that he has to tune in at some point. "I come here for him. The guy that was laughing. He's the baker, I think. Or maybe the owner. He's just... I don't even know. I found out his name the other day. Gage." I shrug, nearly spilling my drink with the motion and setting it down to avoid that happening again. "It's his laugh. I have no clue how someone could possibly be that happy. I feel like, maybe I was there once. Maybe as a kid, before the real world sunk in. I just... it blows my mind that he's so untouched by everything."

I look up and Noah is looking back at me. His green eyes are piercing. Like the ocean during a storm. Cold, harsh, unforgiving. But there is something there behind them too. Curiosity maybe? I decide to keep going. What's the worst that could happen?

"I'm pretty messed up. Just got back from seeing my shrink. Work mandated because I was on leave for a while. Didn't go that well. It never really does. I don't think she actually listens but at the same time she always has an opinion. And it's not always professional." I'm getting a little carried away, I haven't had a good ramble in a while. I shake my head and get to the point, "Look, I guess I'm just sick of being alone. I thought maybe you were to." He is still watching me, not talking, but he seems to be paying attention. It's apparently enough to keep me going today. And on a topic I hadn't really planned on, one that has my voice quieting with nervous energy. "Do you believe in ghosts?"

Noah has every right to be skeptical, but he shrugs, eyes still studying my face and waiting for me to continue. And when I don't continue right away he asks why.

So I tell him.

And he listens.

He asks questions. He talks about the weird dreams the hospital has been giving him and the feeling that he is being watched. He thinks the place could be haunted, but he hasn't ever seen anything to prove it. Definitely not like I was describing, but he doesn't judge either. He is skeptical at worst, but he said he believes me. The feeling that I can open up and it could go well, that someone could believe me, could be on my side, is almost euphoric. It's better than any medication or comfort food or security blanket in the world. Noah tells me I should research them. That I have a way of painting a picture when I talk. He likes this story better than anything he's found in the donated book bin at the hospital. He thinks I could write about them or something. The thought has me practically glowing.

I have always wanted to write. Ever since I was a little girl. I tell him that too. Again, he doesn't judge. There's no talk of, why or more serious careers or full time benefits and livelihood like there had been with Nick. Noah just nods, like it's the obvious choice. Like changing my life would be the simplest thing in the world. He doesn't tell me writing is just a hobby or that I need a real job. He only asks why I became a nurse instead. And he even understands the pressure to be responsible. *Where has this magical person come from?* I ask myself.

He finally starts to talk about himself and then, I get it. He's the big brother. He's been doing it, supporting, all his life. Noah talks about how he gave up everything when their mom died to take care of his little brother. He talks about how he made sure to keep Sam in school and help him get good grades and into a good college. About how he worked close to seventy hour weeks to keep them afloat and make sure that Sam wasn't working too hard while trying to concentrate in school. Because school was supposed to be important. He was raised to believe that if you went to school, you got the good jobs, you got to live your dreams.

But that didn't happen for Sam. And then the drugs happened. Noah was naive enough to think that his baby brother really did find a job with his degree. He trusted him. He didn't think he would ever end up dealing like their father had. "I tried to give him everything. I did some really shitty things to get food on the table. I should be the one that's messed up." He takes a moment, pushing his coffee cup to the side a little too strong, but I let him. "Maybe because I needed to be good for him."

I try reaching across the table to lay one of my hands over his clenched fists. "He has you."

"Yeah, but I'm nothing." Noah leans back in his seat, taking his fists with him. He stares out the window as he continues, venting to the air, but I listen. If it's all I'm allowed to do, it's what I'll do.

Noah blames himself for the fight they had that night. If he hadn't been so mad, if he hadn't dumped the drugs down the sink, if he hadn't been yelling then maybe Sam wouldn't have stormed off. Maybe he wouldn't have met those kids. Maybe if Noah had gone after him, he could have been able to protect his baby brother from getting the brains beat out of him so bad the call in had said Sam had been hit by a car. He could have protected him. It was his job. His career. The only thing that mattered. And he messed it up.

"There's no way you could have known what he was walking into. It sounds like you're a pretty amazing big brother. Mine used to be like that. He's had it rough lately too. He lost his best friend and it was all my fault." I shake my head, I'm not going to make this about me. "Point is, it's not your fault Noah. You're human. You got mad and from the sound of it, you had every right to be mad." But I know how guilt works. I'm not surprised when he gets up and walks out. I just wish that I had seen it coming sooner.

I stay in my seat for a while, listening to the chatter in the back, staring at the ridiculous movie posters on the wall. I'm in the middle of reading the description for this weekend's showing of *'Master of the Flying Guillotine'* when Noah comes back into my line of vision still looking upset, but a little more calm than when he left. Maybe even sheepish.

"I don't know where I am." He mumbles. I can't help the smile that touches my lips. Gage's laughter echoes in the background as we make our way back to the street.

CHAPTER TWELVE

I have the night off to think about my talk with Noah. About how I trusted him with my miserable secret and how he supported me. I know I had craved that but I had no idea how much it would mean to me until it actually happened. I think I owed it to both of us to at least try and look into everything a little more. Or at all honestly, since so far my research had revolved around memories of the horror movies Ted had scared me with when we were younger.

The problem is, I don't exactly know where to start. I can't imagine a google search for shadow monsters going over very well on my psyche. Maybe if I could remember the very first one I had seen...

A flash of a stretched out shadow on the wall in the living room tears through my mind. No, that wasn't them. I don't want to think about that shadow.

Maybe that's why I hate them so much. They're a constant, agonizing reminder.

March 23rd

The street is much longer than I remember as I weave down it, squinting whenever I get too close to one of the blaring blue lights from an emergency call box. I did not feel this tipsy sitting inside Josie's with Courtney.

I finally get back to the apartment, shambling up the three flights to the top, not ashamed to use my hands on the stairs of the last floor no matter how clammy and gritty the ugly speckled gray carpet is. There is no shame at 2 am on a Thursday after pulling three days of doubles to avoid being home. I brace myself on our door frame to dig out my key and catch my breath.

I know it's late but the call of coffee is too strong and by some miracle the pot is still squeaky clean and upside down next to the coffee maker where I had left it this morning. Had hell frozen over? In what realm did Nick actually do the dishes? Either the world was about to end or Nick had done something he was going to ask forgiveness for in the morning. I set the coffee maker up to brew and lean against the counter, dropping my head and cracking my neck from side to side as I take in a noise. There is an odd background noise that is finally registering in my swimming brain. Not a clicking, exactly. More of a creak-click, creak-click, like something is broken or stuck or just annoying as hell. "What is that fucking noise?" I snap at no one, straightening up to dig for a mug in the back of the cupboard I can barely reach. It would be nice if Nick didn't shove them all the way to the back every damn time. What is his obsession with thinking that they are going to fall out of the cupboard? The coffee maker blinks and beeps at me that it has completed its simple task, and I reach over to pull the pot off of the plate so it would stop its touting. Balanced on my toes, one hand to the side holding the steaming pot away from my body and the other as deep in the cupboard as I can reach, I feel something shift in the air.

I felt fine, but… You always feel fine. Right up until the precise moment when you don't. That moment has a chill running up my spine and my face going numb where the blood rushes out of it. It's a few moments right after the metallic clicking becomes all I can hear and it has my fingers going numb around the sharp plastic handle of the coffee pot. I see something move in the corner of my eye and whip my head around to scold Nick for sneaking up on me and demand he reach a mug as penance.

The steaming hot coffee splashes off the floor and onto my shoes, soaking through the canvas, through my socks and scorching my feet, making me drop the pot completely and step back as it shatters.

There is a silhouette against the wall that is all wrong. Shocking and disturbing in its angle and stretched out limbs. Limbs that reached the floor but looked… I turn my head slightly to the left, unable to blink, unable to move anything else.

A car passes on the street and its head lights send a beam of light throughout the room, illuminating the scene in odd flashes through the vertical blinds. I see the ceiling fan, the blades stuck in a repetitive forward-snapback. Forward-snapback. Because something is wrapped up around the motor, crushing the light fixture to tilt them at an awkward angle towards the wall. Because something is pulling it, weighing it down.

Something impossible.

"Nick!"

*****

I snap myself out of the memory with a jolt. That's it. I need to leave this apartment. I end up at the hospital, I don't know where else to go. I walk around aimlessly for a bit, looking for familiar faces and avoiding them all the same.

Something drags me back up to the ICU and Sam's room. Noah looks up when I walk in, rubbing the tiredness from his eyes. "Hey."

"Hi." I say, as if we hadn't just left each other. "I don't know where to start. I can't-" I look up and away, not wanting to get emotional in front of this poor man and possible friend.

Noah gestures to the seat by the window, the one no one ever uses since he has been the only visitor. He pulls out his phone.

"So, shadow people. Yours don't have red eyes do they?" He asks, scratching his head and looking nervous that a red eyed boogie man was about to appear. He started with a goddamn shadow monsters google search. I can't help the dry chuckle that escapes.

"No. Thank whatever god that cares."

Noah huffs his own laugh and we continue on in silence, staring at our phones looking for answers.

Around midnight, I finally find an artist named Oliver Scott. It isn't a perfect portrayal, but it was pretty damn close, a lot closer than anything else we were finding. A picture of a statue on his site actually has a jolt race up my spine. I pass my phone over the bed to show Noah.

"His studio's not that far from here." Is all he says.

"Yeah. I saw." I'm nervous to ask, but the thought of going alone is so much worse. "Do you want to go?" Noah's eyes look down and something dark passes over his face. I regret asking. Still, my hopes betray me by getting themselves all raised. He looks back at Sam.

"Can't. I need to stay here. Don't want him to wake up alone." I nod my head with a smile, getting up to take the phone back. My muscles are stiff from sitting in the crappy chair for so long. I don't know how Noah continues to do it without complaint. Maybe I could have one of the recliners for the spouses who slept over in post-op brought over.

I squeeze his shoulder on my way out. "Okay." I go to leave but stop. "Can I have your phone for a sec?" Noah passes it over and I tap away at the screen, plugging my number into his contacts. "I always answer. I promise. If anything comes up or you change your mind, let me know. Okay?"

He looks at me like I just grew another head. Maybe I had. It would explain why only half of my brain seemed to be working lately.

CHAPTER THIRTEEN

I wait for the next morning to try calling the number for the artist I had hunted down with Noah the night before. I pace nervously through three rings before a throat is clearing on the other end. "Royal Road Psychoanalysis and Counseling Services, Olli speaking." says a voice with a thick brogue.

I freeze. Scottish is a good thing, but I wasn't expecting a doctor's office. "Um... Is this Oliver Scott?"

"Yes..." The voice drags out before he seems to catch on, "Wait, are you calling for me?" He sounds equally confused and excited. This call was not going anywhere near what I had planned. I explain that yes, I am looking for him and want to talk about his work. To say he is ecstatic would be a vast understatement.

"Are you a therapist as well?" I ask nervously. That would be too good to be true. Then again, maybe not. I don't think I want my personal demons, literally or figuratively, to be someone else's muse.

"No, but my fiancé is. My studio is in her office. Not as many people call for me." There was a pause before the dreaded question. "...Did you need that kind of help too, maybe?"

"No, I mean, I have a psychiatrist. But maybe she's not such a great fit. I think I'm looking for someone more open minded."

Oliver hums a chuckle to himself. "Well, I think you've found the right place. Why don't you come down, today's your day off you said? Jae has an open schedule between eleven and three for reschedules and emergencies. Why don't you head over and you can have a chat with the both of us?" When Livia didn't answer right away he was quick to continue. "Or just me. Whatever you're comfortable with."

"That… that actually sounds nice. Thank you."
A few hours later and I am swaying in my seat on the train, trying not to think about being enclosed in such a small space with so many people and their shadows, regular and otherwise.

*****

"I mean, obviously I believe in them." Oliver says gesturing to the statue in the center of his studio located in the back of the counseling offices and what looks like their home together. A curved wall of windows shines natural light onto paintings dry and wet alike. They are all beautiful and so much more detailed than their pictures online. Oliver on the other hand is not what I had expected at all.

I was picturing the Hollywood portrayal of an artist. Black turtleneck, slicked back hair, pale and thin, maybe a splash of paint conveniently highlighting one of his better features. Not Oliver. His shock of red hair is a mess of curls and knots that are matted with paint, a traditionally woman's hairclip or two keeping some it off his forehead. He is in a worn thin flannel over a shamelessly splattered t-shirt and jeans that looked as though they have been used to wipe off a potter's wheel. It was definitely less intimidating than what I had been picturing on the train ride over, that's for sure.

"My gran, she used to tell me all these stories about them after her husband died. She really missed him. I'll never get why, he was a right bastard. Cheated on her all the time and didn't bother to hide it. I learned later he'd beat her too. Real arsehole with a lot of darkness in his heart. But sometimes, no matter how much it hurts you, you can't help who you love, right?"

"Wow, hope you're not talking about me there Olli." A smoky voice says from the doorway. I turn to see a striking woman, the opposite of Oliver in every possible way. Her hair is dark and neat, tucked into a smart bun, and a chic sweater dress is hugging her curves. But most noticeably, she has two different color eyes. One is an electric shade of blue, the other a deep brown, with just a lightning strike matching the other eye at the top. Still, there is something warm and inviting about her, professional as her air may seem, she projects kindness and acceptance.

"Actually, I was getting around to you. Got a little distracted though love." Oliver beams at her, clearly head over heels. "Livia, this is Jaeli Tal, Jae, this is the lovely Miss Livia Moss. She came to ask me about my muse." He elbows the statue as if it's an old buddy. "I was just going to recommend she speak with you for a bit though. She's feeling down lately. And she recognized my work as something that's been popping up in her life a bit." The artist raises his eyebrows meaningfully as if the words weren't enough. Livia likes him, it's impossible not to.

"Oh, well hello Miss Moss." Jaeli winks at Oliver. "I told you." Some inside joke passes between them that catches my interest.

"Yeah, yeah. I should know by now not to bet against you woman."

I'm about to ask, but I'm too quickly swept up in a conversation with both of them about what I have been seeing. Soon enough I have an appointment with Jaeli for my next day off to discuss my dreams and the possibility of more appointments.

"I know it's a bit of a hoof for you," Oliver tells me on my way out, "but if it works, won't it be worth it?"

I can't help but agree. I have a good feeling about this place.

*****

When I get home, I continue my day off on the research trail. It's too late to try and accomplish anything else, at least that's what I tell myself. That and I've met my socialization quota for the day between the train and the new shadow I have on my heels. It's a tall one with hunched shoulders and a bit of an attitude problem. At least it seems to be shy enough not to get too close.

I find myself scrolling though site after site about dream research. I learn about the common meanings of this or that detail I can remember. I find out that you're not supposed to dream of faces that you don't already know. I find ways to know you're dreaming while still within the dream. Like not being able to understand numbers or letters. I think, maybe if I can recognize these while I'm having a nightmare, then I can pull myself out of it. The method seems to work for some bloggers.

Most of the sites that hit home with me are the blogs. The personal experiences. Some of them are set up just for the scare factor, announcing ghost stories of the week or guaranteed nightmares.

Some are research into the paranormal. Some are people looking for help. What I notice though, are that all bloggers, no matter what their main focus is, are commenting and making friends within this community, sharing experiences and comparing notes. I don't think it's such a bad idea.

A couple more hours of scrolling and I'm creating my own *tumblr*, laughing on the inside at the David Bowie reference in my title as I hum 'Golden Years' to myself and type up the "About Me".

> *It doesn't matter what is real to anyone else, if you see it than it is real to you. I see shadows and I am trying to figure out why and what they are. Be it some psychic episode, chemical imbalance or trauma induced illusion I just want to know. And I want to know if anyone else is seeing something similar. Please make use of my ask and submit links to share your stories. Thank you.*

I don't think it's too bad for my first step into the blogging world. I decide to continue with a first post and try my best to describe what I'm seeing. Luckily, I have a model hanging about, if I can count having a shadow monster in my room as lucky. Unluckily, the combination of having said model in the room and thinking about the topic enough to write on it is giving me the heebie jeebies. I'm not going to sleep any time soon. Not that I could with an audience anyway.

I see shadows. Solid shadows. Solid shadows shaped like people...

It sounds crazy, I know it does, but they're there so what do you do about that? Get psychiatric help? Seek medical attention? Done it. And these...things don't fit into any psychiatric or medical category. Having an older brother with a taste for sci-fi and horror movies—it wasn't hard to become terrified by what might be an answer. But even looking into alternate avenues and paranormal research, I have yet to find a definition that completely encompasses my experience.

WHAT I SEE:

Shape: My shadows are of humanoid shape. They differ in height but not too drastically. Most seem to be around my height [5'6"] or taller. Rarely are they shorter, but it has occurred. None have been less than approximately 5 feet.

Color: They are solid black but sometimes, with movement, can be translucent at the edges. Kind of like a lagging image, but more so like what you would see if someone were to wear loose clothing of a light material. The translucent part of them is dark in color as well and looks more like your typical object-between-light source-and-wall shadow.

Features: I cannot discern a face or any features, though they do differ in height, build and [I guess you could call it] personality/attitude. [More on that later]. Their body appears to be cloaked as do their heads and faces. I say cloaked but it's like one solid shape over them. It's really hard to explain and I wish I could draw. It's kind of like when an artist drapes fabric over a whole piece if that makes any sense, but it's a part of them. Like they walked through it and it flows with them. It's actually quite graceful and would maybe be beautiful if it weren't so terrifying. The term "through the veil"

73

comes to mind but I'll refrain from puns. They do have hands. The hands are long, though not necessarily inhumanly so, thin, solid black, and have no discernible features like nails, lines, wrinkles etc. Sometimes feet are discernible, also humanoid.

I paste a few pictures of what I've been able to find that are close and write little comments on what I would change. After I post it, I put together another post full of Oliver's art and a blurb about getting to talk to him and how I think his muse might be what I'm seeing, but that the artist has never seen one himself. I think that's enough for one night.

I shut down the computer and stretch. I still don't feel much like sleeping yet. Miracle of miracles. It must have been a combination of the scary stories I had found and having completed something. Especially having *written* something that I really enjoyed writing after so long without my old favorite hobby. I decide to tidy up the laundry pile on my desk and make sure none of the mail next to it is anything that needs to go back anytime soon. I find the mail caddy I had bought when I moved in to keep my mail separate from Nicks' that I had never hung up. Now was as good a time as any. Maybe it would help me to be a bit more organized.

A girl can dream.

CHAPTER FOURTEEN

I *see myself sleeping and I watch. Watch the slow rising and falling of my chest. Watch the stirs in the blanket around my feet. I move around the room, viewing a sleeping me from every angle, bored and perplexed.*

Nothing is happening outside the little bedroom window. There rarely ever is. I make my way back to the foot of the bed. I reach out a dark finger and poke the feet still stirring there. I watch myself twitch and get a sense of amusement. That I can still reach out. Touch. Have some kind of impact on the world. Even if it isn't positive.

I turn to face the desk and have a seat on the bed, those feet twitching away from me again.

There's a notebook here. Pens and markers too. Everything has a fine sheen of dust and specks of laundry lint over it, but I'm not bothered.

I ignore the list started at the top of the page, pick up a pen and start to write.

The words flow easily, in a practiced, pretty cursive unlike my usual scrawl. Bold and neat, tilted to the right and far more legible than what I'm used to. "We were best friends," I write. It takes me a while to add more. Guilt and grief rolling the acid in my belly and boiling my blood. Making its pulse pound through my head in a dizzying beat. "and I loved him." The period is a violent stab, but after the ink bleeds out of the little dot I feel a stress release unlike any other. I feel like I can breathe again at the admission and the writing starts to flow faster. "We were practically inseparable for twenty years, Will and I. Best friends. Confidants. Brothers, not by blood shared but in blood spilt from scrapped knees and ill thought out adventures.

"Then Amelia. My father arranged a place at her family's dinner table for me but I would have done anything not to go. Dragging a sputtering Will along seemed like the best course of action at the time.

"At least until his small town charm was casting a spell on the girl's parents and unfortunately, Amelia herself.

"Next thing I know, she's enrolled in all the classes we share. Bonding with Will, my Will, over Shakespeare and Vol-taire. Helping him write essays. Partnering with him in chem-istry. He would never read poems with me. Always copied my notes. Wasn't even going to go to college until I begged him.

"Suddenly he's a scholar.

"Then, Christmas break comes along and so does a ring. That thing we both swore we'd never do. What I thought we'd never do for the same reason. Because we couldn't.

"I don't go to the engagement party. Can't. I foolishly stay home where I know he'll come looking for me eventually. Be-cause he's my friend. Just friend. Best friend. Because if your best friend doesn't show up at your engagement party, some-thing has to be wrong.

"We sit together on the porch. Listen to the cicadas and the bats. The cows mooing and chewing. Watch the fireflies glow and disappear as we drink the beers I pinch from the fridge.

"I want to tell him so badly.

"Don't marry her. I know your secret. It's mine too. Don't do it to make anyone happy but yourself. Right now, like this, you're not happy. You can't be. You're not even you.

"But I can't. My dad and little sister are just a screen door away. And I'm not positive that Will isn't happy. And he never actually told me any secret like that. Maybe it was just wishful thinking on my part that thought his stares were a little too long or that sometimes his hand brushed mine when it didn't have to.

"This little, guilty voice in the back of my head tells me he could never love me, he really was happy, it was just me being jealous.

"So I started ignoring him. I didn't go back to school. At least, not ours. I wanted to be a writer. Live in a city with a his-tory and exciting people to inspire me. Wanted to be the next

Vonnegut. Had this story all mapped out in my head about a man who falls in love with a ghost he can never touch.

"But I can never finish it. "They say write what you know, but that just hurts too much sometimes.

"I have my fancy New England education and papers to prove it, but I can't make the rent work if the ink won't flow and what does isn't published. I have to go home. But it doesn't mean I have to see him. Or her and her chubby little girl picking out watermelon and tomatoes at the farmer's market. Will hated tomatoes. But he loved watermelon. Could cut one in half and sit on the steps scooping out bite after bite all day. Or licking the juices from his wrist and sucking them off his fingers if Ma ever cut us some for lunch.

"When hiding in my old room full of memories and missed mail doesn't work I decide to take up the family business for a few months. At least until my dad catches me drunk off my mind with a guy in a bar bathroom and it was move out or sign up like the old man. Learn discipline. Thought I raised you right. So I joined up. Because home didn't feel like home anymore without Will, and even though a new town with a better view and bigger, better farmer's market sounded like exactly what I wanted, maybe dad was right and a little action was what I needed. Turns out it didn't matter, because either way I never got to come back. Never got to see those blue eyes spark from hidden laughter because of me. Or see that bitten smile while he tried to behave. Never got to tell him or apologize for telling him or kiss him if by some miracle he felt the same. Never got to try "

The sentence hangs like that, no period, no comma. No ending or maybes. I throw the pen against the wall and whip around to slap the feet toeing at me. I want to be alone. I want to go home. If only I knew where that was.

****

I wake up with a jerk. The kind that feels like you're dropping out of the sky back into bed. My feet are freezing and I find the shiver running from my toes right up my back. I send a cursory glance around the room, making sure that none of the shadows around me are the moving kind before getting out of bed to check the thermostat. I pause by my desk, running a hand over the dusty note book.

Everything looks just like it did in my dream, except there's no new writing under my work schedule and half thought out grocery list.

A bright zap of static stings my finger when it dares to touch the metal spiral of the notebook and my heart ticks up a beat from the surprise.

"I thought you weren't supposed to be able to read in dreams." I mumble to myself, shuffling off to bump the heat up a couple degrees.

CHAPTER FIFTEEN

Things stay the same for a little while. Not getting any better, but not getting worse either. Work is mundane, the blog slowly garners a following but no results, and Noah continues to poke at different research pages between rereading magazines and playing different games on his phone from Sam's side. The train ride back to Jaeli and Oliver's offices is nerve wracking. It feels like meeting them for the first time all over again, only this time I am paying Jaeli to analyze me. Why am I doing this again? It's not like the woman could actually help. I have been walking the fence between crazy and haunted for so long, but now I'm really starting to believe. After what I have read and what I've been seeing, these things might just be real. And how could a therapist help with that? The best I could hope for was getting better sleep if Jaeli has some insight into my dreams.

When I finally get off the stuffy, overcrowded morning train, I find the walk through the neighborhood refreshing. It's a college block, much nicer than mine. It isn't long before I can see the tree with the pink flowers on the corner next to the brownstone I am looking for. I see Oliver in the corner window in front of an easel, staring out the glass into space. I try to wave but he's in an artist's trance. Not even the shrill doorbell disturbs him. Soon enough Jaeli is ushering me in, showing me the waiting room where I had talked with them last time, and telling me that I could come right in and wait next time. Their door is always open. Only the upstairs is off limits.

I think that's a little too trusting for city dwellers but I suppose that's how a regular office would be run. A home office really shouldn't be any different.

We settle in on chairs in a little room off to the side, Jaeli turning on a white noise machine and classical music outside the door before we go in. She gestures for me to pick a seat before grabbing a clipboard and choosing the armchair across from me.

"I hope you don't mind, but I'd like to get a feel for where you are today by asking about your dreams. Do you remember what you dreamt last night?" She asks, putting her pen on the arm of the chair and folding her hands over her note pad. That was refreshing. Maybe she would be more interested in what I had to say and less in her short hand or doddles or whatever it was Dr. Baron is always scratching away at.

"I do, but I had a couple of questions about that. If it's okay?" I say, my hands hovering between a surrender motion and finding a place on my lap. I'm ridiculously nervous that I will offend my new therapist so quickly. Dr. Baron hated it it when I tried to control the conversation.

"Absolutely. What's on your mind?"

I take a deep breath, attempting not to try so hard. This woman is different, I needed to get over it. "Well, I've been doing some research. About dreams and what I've been dreaming specifically. In your experience, do people often dream of faces they've never seen and places they've never been? I mean, I've always had a vivid imagination," I say with an eye roll, thinking of Ted, "but according to my research I'm not supposed to dream about people I don't know."

"Hmm. That's a tough question to answer. Especially with the reason you're here." Jaeli seems to think for a moment, slipping the clipboard between the cushion and the arm of her chair and stretching her legs out to rest her feet up on the coffee table. "No, you're generally not supposed to dream of faces you haven't seen, but there are exceptions to every rule. Some people are more sensitive to the world around them. You could be dreaming of background faces you never consciously recognized or noticed. Or old school mates you don't remember. On the other hand, you seem to believe in the existence of the supernatural, therefore you could be having some sort of psychic episode-"

"You seriously think that could be happening?" I interrupt, shocked that a doctor would even consider the realm of the supernatural as an actual answer.

"I *seriously think* that you're experiencing something that medicine has failed to assist you in. That is if you're still taking what you wrote here regularly?" I nod. I haven't liked it or benefited from it that I could tell, but I have been taking them every night just in case there was a sliver of a chance things could change. "I think that if you're open to the idea and we're looking into the possibility of ghosts then no stone should be left unturned."

I feel a weight lift off my shoulders that I hadn't realized I'd carried here. I am actually being taken seriously. It shouldn't be such a foreign concept, but I'm dumbfounded by it.

"Can I answer anything else for you? Or would you like to tell me about the faces in your dreams?"

"Just one more thing. You're not supposed to be able to read or count either, right? Because I can. I mean, I can read. I haven't tried to count yet."

"That's interesting." Jeali seems serious, as if she's excited to hear more, not as if I'm some science experiment. "Are you sure you're reading, or is your dream sort of..." Jeali moves her hands in front of her looking for the phrase, "translating an understanding for you."

"No. I, okay. A few nights ago, most of my dream was me sitting down writing a story I had never heard about these people I've never known in some backwoods part of the country I've never been to. It was just me, at my desk in front of a note book with my old work schedule on it writing like it was a journal. My whole dream was words and sometimes snippets of the faces of the people I was writing about or emotions or whatever. But mostly just the words being written. Only, the hand and the handwriting wasn't mine. And when I woke up, I went to the notebook and it was in the same place with the same words on it only the story was missing. That's weird, right?"

Jaeli nods slowly, eyes wide and excited. "That's amazing. I've never heard of that happening before. I'm not claiming to be the topmost expert on dream analysis, but it is my concentration and I can say with certainty that what you experienced is definitely not what the general public sees when they sleep."

"What do you think it means?"

"I honestly have no idea. But I would love to try and figure that out with you. Can you remember any details of the story you wrote? Or maybe we should start with the handwriting. Was it familiar? Any particular color of ink or style that speaks to you or niggles at a memory?"

We go on, analyzing step by step of what I can remember. It's tedious and frustrating at points. I don't know what these things mean to her. It feels like they belonged to someone else, but if it helped than I owed it to myself to give it a try.

Eventually we get around to the shadows, Jaeli perfectly calm with the possibility of a demon or ghoul or whatever haunting her office.

"Why don't you try talking to them? A real conversation, not just a dismissal. Is there one here right now? Where is he or she, no offense buddy." Jaeli says, glancing around the room as if she could spot it if she tried hard enough.

"I can't. I don't…. it's easier when you can't see them I guess."

"You shouldn't judge a beast by its shadow, Livia. We don't know what they are yet. I'm not saying to go out and get a Ouija board, you don't need any more issues right now that those can bring up, paranoia or paranormal. But maybe just talk, if not to them than *at* them? Or try?"

"I do sometimes. If they're being really bad."

"Maybe they just want attention. Maybe they're excited you can see them or they don't understand why and are trying to give you a message. Just something to think about, okay?"

I nod, just because I would think about it didn't mean I have to do it.

We end up talking about the blogs I'd discovered for the last few minutes of the session and how I have started my own. Jaeli warns me about putting up a disclaimer. That it was okay to talk to people about the issues we were dealing with, but I didn't want to be seen as responsible for solving or causing their problems. It wasn't a bad idea.

I think about bringing up the guilt that weighs me down every day. But Jaeli's been so helpful and understanding. I don't want her pity and I don't want to take her entire day.

Later, I tell myself. I still have Dr. Baron to help with that for now. It's easier with someone who already knows everything than having to explain again from the start.

*****

When I get home I trip over my shoes for the last time. *That is it! It's not like they were actually barricading the door against things that could just appear or whatever they did anyway. It was time to un-nest. I'd had it.*

"This isn't an invitation, okay? I just need to not break my neck every time I have to get up to pee." I announce to what I hope is no one and get out my laptop to find a shoe rack.

I feel good about it. It's nice to accomplish something, no matter how small. To see a change you've made in the world, even if it's just your own world.

CHAPTER SIXTEEN

"Hey you. Anything new?" I ask as I swing into the room ignoring Dementor Dickwad stationed in the corner trying to click to the beat of Sam's respirator. What a jerk.

Noah just shakes his head, twisting a fork through the lime Jell-O someone must have slipped him. She checks her watch, he must have been playing with that cup for hours. She's surprised it wasn't soup by now. Then again, there really isn't anything like hospital Jell-O.

"Well I had an interesting day." I say, going to the chair on the other side of Sam's bed. I straighten his hair and warm his hand in mine, flexing his sleeping muscles. The nurse on duty, Kim as the whiteboard says, has most likely already run through Sam's PT for the afternoon but a little extra wouldn't hurt. "Had my first session with the therapist that specializes in dreams and she thinks I'm seeing spirits or whatever. I like her. Definitely better than Grumpy Cat in the offices across the street. At least she has some personality. That train ride though." I shake my head. I don't know how much longer I can carry the conversation. Socializing was exhausting enough, never mind when you had to do all the work. "Yeah. Anyway, she seems nice. Not as judgmental as you'd think. Still, I don't know how much she can help. It's not like anyone has any experience in my brand of crazy."

"I don't think you're crazy."

"And I love you for that. But I kind of am. For an example, if I may. Do you see anyone right now? Hear anyone? Sense anything?" Noah just raises his eyebrows at me. Answer

84

enough. "I do. Dickwad, my personal favorite, is right next to me. Being a dickwad. Actually, I think I'm going to change his name to Vader. He's a real heavy breather." I look right at the monster, hoping to elicit some kind of silence from him. Nothing. "Hopefully he doesn't learn how to do a Force Choke anytime soon. I'm pretty sure I'll be his first target if he gets all dark side." Noah just rolls his eyes, going back to playing with the green mush, "No? Nothing? Not a Star Wars fan?"

"You name them?"

"Why not? It's easier than thinking of them as skinny, shorty, the only nice one, and evil bastards four, five, and six."

"I'm sorry."

I glare at him, "This is in no way your fault. And unfortunately there's nothing you can do. I'm stuck in a world of nightmares and ghosties. At least I have you to talk to about it now. And Jaeli, though I pay her so I'm not sure that counts."

"You don't have anyone else?"

"Well, I'm never alone. But yeah, just me and my shadows." I'm hilarious, I don't understand how Noah can be so impervious to my wit. He digs in his pocket and pulls out a well-loved lighter. He brushes a piece of lint off and chucks it over. I barely catch it in my surprise.

"My mom gave that to me. She said it was for when the light at the end of the tunnel goes out." I look down at it. At the little scrapes where the color has worn off and the faded logo of a B that once declared Noah a Boston Red Sox fan to anyone who saw him using it. There are little bits of paper stuck to it, like maybe it had once been covered in stickers. This thing is old, and from what he said about how he practically raised his brother, I am guessing his mom gave it to him too long ago for me to be able to accept this.

"Noah, this is great, but-"

"I've been lighting it every night out in the courtyard with the smokers. I'd light it in here but..." Noah trails off as he gestures to the oxygen in use sign. "Doesn't seem to be lighting my way right now. But it might help you. Just give it back when you don't need it anymore okay? At least I've got Sam. Sounds like you could use it more."

"I can't."

"Yeah you can."

I tap my nail against the rusty wheel. "Alright. On one condition." Noah looks up at me, an eyebrow raised in question.

"What's that?"

I let the smile creeping onto my lips take over. "Pizza. Right now. You and me. We can even bring it back here if you want but you need some more fresh air."

"Hear that Sammy? Your favorite nurse over there is sick of your ugly mug." Vader doesn't seem so pleased about us getting up to leave, but as I put the lighter in my pocket and give it a pat, I can't quite bring myself to care. Nothing changes on the monitors when Noah jokes at his brother and gives his shoulder a punch goodbye. I don't know if it's hope or denial, but I just want to hold my new friend tight, keep him together. But how am I supposed to do that when I'm cracking at the slightest bit of pressure myself?

We spend a few hours just talking. Shooting the shit. Telling stories about growing up with brothers and dealing with the bullshit that is their lives. I can't believe that after so many years, I finally have a friend that seems to understand me. It feels nice to have that again. And terrifying, knowing I could lose the new friendship at any minute for any reason.

Still, I make it my goal to get a smile out of him tonight and I succeed, albiet briefly, a few times before the bill comes.

I offer up my couch to him when we leave, lecturing him about sleeping in the ridiculously uncomfortable hospital chairs but Noah turns me down on the corner where I need to turn left for home and he heads back to sneak into Sam's room even though visiting hours are long over. I shake my head to hide the disappointment.

Pro : he won't be subjected to one of my crazy nightmares and the subsequent paranoia and/or screaming that would most likely occur.

Con : I'm going home to a not so empty apartment, alone again.

I flick the stiff wheel of the lighter and feel the heat of the flame dance over my thumb. Little sparks wisp around the yellow glow, and the blue and white center mesmerizes me for a minute before it's too hot to keep lit. I can't help the corner of my mouth ticking up at someone caring enough to help me like this. I pocket the lighter again and play with it in my pocket as I continue on my way.

CHAPTER SEVENTEEN

I wake up from a peacefully dreamless sleep from the feeling of cold, darkness settling in all around me. "Now? Really? It's bed time. Are all of you nocturnal? How do you have the energy to follow me around all day and keep watch at night?" I mumble, my eyes start to droop again but the slim shadow jerks closer. "You're the one that lays here sometimes. Right? Grumpy?" I think I must be going mad but remembered Jaeli. Remembered the woman's conviction, con idence and bravery. *I can do this.* Grumpy jerks himself into reclining next to me and reaches out a draped hand, pausing before touching me this time. In my half asleep state, I have the courage to reach back.

*****

I wake up in a room of white light. Nothing for miles and miles but light. I look down at my uniform. I'm some kind of soldier. No. I'm a Ranger. The lights start to go out one by one, chasing me down the white hallway until there's nothing. Nowhere. I see nothing. I hear nothing. I am nothing. Except... I can still feel.

Hate
I can taste it. Gritty and metallic, like sandy blood bubbling up in my mouth.

Faces flash before my eyes. I promised to bring my best friend back from the desert. Not to get him shot saving my useless ass. I hate that everyone forgives me before I even tell them what happened. I don't deserve their forgiveness. I don't deserve them.

I squeeze my eyes shut against the burning rage in the back of my throat. When I open them, I'm back in that familiar but unfamiliar hospital room. Maggie is holding my hand. Her eyes as wet as mine feel. And I just know it, she's pregnant. She's happy somehow. I can't understand that.

"He's still with us this way Manny. It's a miracle." It's not. It's something else I took away from him.

"I promised to bring him home-" My voice cracks in a tone not at all mine.

"You did."

"It wasn't supposed to be in a box, Maggie!" That look crossed her face again. That one I can't read, but I'm pretty sure I know what it means. Disappointment. I deserve every bit of that.

"We weren't going to try until he was home for good. He is now. It's a sign. A miracle."

I can't look at her. I don't hear her leave, but I know I'm alone. Utterly and completely alone.

The guilt is too much. It clogs my throat, presses on my chest, blurs my eyes, claws at my guts and leaves me carved out and empty. Darkens my days into endless nights. Into that long, dark hallway.

My cast comes off and my leg looks brand new. Barely a scar. I hate it. I hate that it's still even attached after its betrayal. I hate that I barely need physical therapy because everyone thinks I'm strong.

I'm not.

I'm weak.

I'm nothing.

I hate my nights. Dreams turning into flashbacks. Literally flashing in my eyes until I wake.

I hate when my dad wakes me up and I pin him to the floor. My father. Black and blue and limping at my hands.

I hate what a failure I am. That I couldn't see the rocks coming. That I couldn't just make it over a damn mountain when all we did as kids was hike them and make it back home before the street lights came on.

That's it. It's my fault. It's all my damn fault that Shawn is dead.

Lights flicker before my eyes as the hall turns into a road and I drive to the reservoir. The one where we tied our bikes to trees and threw each other off cliffs into the crystal lake before drying off climbing the trails.

I park. Run my hand over the old stereo. It's playing that idiot band Shawn and Maggie had their first dance to while I jeered from the sidelines. I shouldn't have stuck around. They'd have been better off if I had just left. Better late than never.

My Desert Eagle's in the glove box.

Just one more song. I'm so sorry. I open the compartment.

The dark hallway surrounds me again. I can hear still. My father, Maggie, people I know and those just pretending to have known us for the juicy details to add to their gossip. People asking why? How could I? Didn't I see?

I can't see.

But I can still hate.

Hate myself for the grief I caused others. Hate that I'm stuck here with this sleeping fool but that I can't ever see dad or Mags or the baby. Hate that I'll never know if it was a boy or girl or its name.

Hate.

Hate.

Hate.

I hate everything. Myself. Fate. My choices. They trapped me here. And there's nothing I can do about it. But hate. I'm just so angry. At the world. At nothing.

Angry at the other shadows. Angry at this bitch for getting to see them, to see what's next and doing nothing to change it. Angry that I didn't get the opportunity to see and to choose.

Angry at myself.

But most of all I'm so afraid. Why did I do it? How could I make such a mistake?

*****

I wake slowly this time to tears dripping down my cheeks, a damp pillow, and static rolling up my fingers where my hand is still in Grumpy's.

"Oh." I sniff and wipe my face with my free hand, not ready to let go yet. Not ready to loose what's dancing on the very tip of my tongue.

Something inside me reaches out and touches where Grumpy's face should be, like I can wipe away its tears too.

In my mind a face appears. Familiar and clear even though I'm sure I've never seen it.

It was me. Dream me. No, him. Manny.

"Holy shit."

CHAPTER EIGHTEEN

Work is easy to go to this morning. It's something to get me away from home. Something to get my mind off the realization that these things, these creatures might just be people. It's too much. It isn't fair that people can do this to me. Could scare me and stalk me and take over my life and my emotions like they were puppet strings to tug this way and that. I've known for a long time that people did monstrous things, but it was something else to BE an actual monster.

I do my rounds. A teenager comes in with burns of such a severity I've never seen outside of text books and television. It's easy to get lost in someone needing my help to that extent. In the thankfulness of his mother and the stern, worried love of his father. I have popped in on Noah and Sam, following my schedule, checking vitals and sneaking Noah bites to eat but I find myself busy to the point where we don't get the chance to really talk until after I clock out and make my way back up to check on them.

I haven't seen Noah in such bad shape since those first couple of weeks.

"Zero brain function. No change. Just more swelling." He mutters when I kneel in front of him to meet his downcast eyes. "The bastards asked about taking him off life support." I'm not surprised. Sam has been in this state for a while now. He is deteriorating in front of his big brother's eyes.

"And?" I ask. I have never seen Noah so unmoved on the subject.

"Fuck you, you know I'm not doing that. He's going to come back. He always was a stupidly deep sleeper." I smile at the tiny spark of his personality shining through. "I just didn't think it would be this long. I'm useless against this."

I squeeze Noah's knee and stand to lean against the end of the bed. I pick up the chart there to flip through it. I know what it says, had added notes to it a couple of hours before. Still, it felt like all I could do and I needed to do something.

"What do you think? Honestly?"

I look back to him and meet piercing green eyes targeting mine. "Honestly, I don't know Noah. I've only ever seen one person come out of a state like this and they hadn't been," How could I put this gently, "inactive for nearly as long as Sam has. It was four days, I think. Back when I was still in school. Take that as you will. It could be a sign of hope. Someone came back. Sam could come back." I put the chart down, taking my eyes away for the next part. "Or it could be a bit of the confirmation you need to feel like you can let him be at peace."

Noah scoffs. I knew he would. "How would you take it?"

I sit back down in the chair on the other side of the bed and take Sam's hand as was routine. "You know me too well by now to think I'm a hopeful person. But you are. So don't let me change you. Okay?

We don't talk much after that. Noah is trapped in his own world. Guilt probably circling his mind that I don't have the slightest idea of how to stop. I try to get him to come back to the apartment for dinner, go out to a restaurant, a bar, whatever he wanted. But it isn't going to happen tonight.

I make my way home, breathing in the chilly evening air and trying to relax before facing my demons. Something catches my eye as I'm getting my keys out at the door. Not uncommon these days.

I look up and Vader is waiting for me in the living room window. I was wondering why it wasn't at the hospital. Still, I don't think I'm ready to face it, him, her, whatever yet. I could use a pick me up before that particular feat.

I head back down the block and cross over to head towards Grind House. I almost lose my nerve when I see Gage wiping down tables instead of in his usual place behind the counter or in the kitchen. But I can't go home. Not yet. I pick up my water and muffin then settle into a corner near the movie board. Apparently this week's feature was *Thriller*. I have enough thrills, thanks.

"Blueberry huh? How'd you like the pumpkin and cranberry yesterday?" I look up and freeze.

"Uh, great. Yeah. Delicious." I nod. I don't think I've blinked once. Oh god, I'm such a freak, I just need to stop blushing and blink. Gage flashes those brilliant teeth at me and sits down.

I am not prepared for this.

Yet, somehow, he is so easy to talk to. It starts with my favorite pastries then, what I do and why I never get coffee. That one I fib through a little though. He seems to notice but it doesn't throw him off. Soon enough I'm venting like he was my oldest friend. I tell him about Noah and Sam. About losing Nick and how I don't know what to do. That I can see myself in Noah and just want to help. That I can't even help myself, how can I possibly help someone else?

My heart practically glows when he says my name with a smile, like he is happy to say it. I hate my name. It's ridiculous. Why couldn't I have just had an O in front? I would have given anything when I was a kid to just be a Jen or Danielle or Mary. At least people would know how to spell and say it. But Gage seemed to genuinely love it. Or maybe he just thought it was funny. I'm fine with that so long as it keeps him smiling.

He is magic. It doesn't hurt to talk with Gage. It feels like breathing after being under water for too long. I'm barely avoiding telling him about my personal haunting, but I can't believe what these patient, dark eyes draw out of me. He must be thinking I am insane. But it doesn't stop him from talking back.

"We carry this guilt. And I do think it's guilt, what you're talking about with your friends. Like, I lost my family pretty young. All of them. It was a house fire, an accident. I was at college, because I couldn't get a flight back for Thanksgiving break. I was the only one not there that night. And I, just for years, I couldn't do anything. Thought if I was sad, I wasn't sad enough, or if I was happy I didn't deserve to be, and it just, it ate at me." Gage is solemn, eyes overcast with an old grief I have never seen touch his features before. It breaks my heart. "We can't just hold ourselves hostage for what's happened to us. We should live. And they'd want that. For us. The people we've lost."

"I-" I have to swallow around the lump in my throat, this bubble of hope I didn't think I was capable of having anymore. I don't know what to say. How he's touched on everything I have been feeling and he is everything I wanted and everything I want to be. I can't believe it is possible for someone like me to become someone like him. To be a ball of sunshine in a business he owned and loved. It seemed so impossible just minutes ago, but now? Hope. I forgot I could even feel that. It was warm. Nice. "Thank you."

"Anytime" he winks as he gets up and makes his way back to the counter.

I walk calmly home in the peace and quiet, cold air of Boston after ten on a random Wednesday night. When I get home, it is to an empty house. For the first time in longer than I would like to admit, I have no trouble falling asleep.

****

When I wake up, it's to a world that's familiar in enough ways that I know I'm home, but not in so many that I know something's wrong. Still, I get up and go out like every morning. I check the coop for eggs and feed the pigs while trying not to think of old Chaunette and the fate that Joanna faces soon and her piglets after that. The sooner I finish my chores, the faster I can make it down the hill and over the fence towards the field the boys have been playing baseball in. I may not be the next Babe Ruth but I'm not afraid to hurt my hand catching and I sure can run and slide. Babe was a traitor anyway, I didn't want to be like him. Even if I didn't mind one bit when Guido gave me the same nick name and it had my uncle rearing.

Banned from baseball or not—I wasn't leaving my boys and I wasn't missing a game. What else was there to do in this boring old town anyway? Carve buttons? Make purses? No thanks. I'm not one to sit around and do nothing all day. I'd rather feel the sun. Rather get dizzy scrubbing bleach into my skirt later just for the chance to smell the grass when I'm rolling down the hill and to the freedom of the game.

I wake up with a jolt. I felt someone grab my leg, I know it, but I'm too afraid to look. It's dark now, too dark to see, barely enough light from the lamp outside peeking in through the shade. But I can feel it still. A weight at the end of my bed. I slowly creep my hand out into the dark, feeling around for the phone. I know it's somewhere on the bed. The longer it takes, the faster my heart beats in my ears. When I finally touch plastic, I cling to it, holding it to my chest and swiping frantically to bring up the light.

Nothing. No shadow. No monsters.

I curl back up in my covers, pulling them higher and tighter this time. I fight sleep as best I can. Shaking my head when my eye lids get too heavy. I turn on the flashlight on my phone and set it beside me, not liking the idea of going back into the dark or sitting up to tug on the light. Even if they were just people, it's still creepy.

Between one heavy blink and the next, I feel the weight again, but this time I can't move. It doesn't matter.

I'm already out of bed.

I'm waving good bye to the pig on the back of the truck. Looking at the empty stall next to the one with the piglets. I'm running away down the hill in a grass stained skirt. I'm hitting a ball through the back window of the pharmacy on Artic Avenue. I'm proud. None of the boys could ever hope to hit that far, but they start to run and it's not fun anymore.

I'm scared.

I'm running and running with them, until they're running ahead and I can't keep up. Guido's calling back to me. But I'm stuck, a hand tight around my arm. "Run!" I yell. And my uncle starts hitting me.

I'm crying in the empty stall again. No, an empty room in a big arm chair. No, it's the empty stall. Or... am I in the room thinking of that empty stall? My hands are wrinkled, knuckles all gnarled. Guido was supposed to be back by now. Where is he? Where am I?

*****

When I wake up, the smaller shadow is perched on the corner of my bed again, staring at my window like she could see right through the shade.

This one was used to sitting. All she ever did later in life at the nursing home was sit and stare in a room by herself. I don't know how someone so adamant on breaking the rules and running with boys, seeing the world and never working in a mill could turn into stone. But when Mae ducks her head and tilts it up slowly like maybe she's giving a shy smile under that void of darkness, I start to understand. I think I get it.

They're just people. They're just *human*. Full of mistakes and regrets and guilt and darkness. Just like me.

I am starting to understand, but hell if I knew what to do.

Chapter Nineteen

"I just... I feel like I'm supposed to be doing something. Like, I hated them. And I'm still afraid kind of. But I think, I'm starting to understand what they are, or at least why they're here. And maybe I'm supposed to do something with that. I just don't know what. What could I possibly do for these people?"

Jaeli is sitting across from me, feet propped up on the coffee table, mug in hand and as smug as could be. "I am so proud of you. I don't think you realize what a huge accomplishment you've made. You're doing what you need to be doing, Livia. There's no need to take on more than you can handle. I think anything else would be a bigger responsibility than you're prepared for right now. But in time, who knows. Maybe you'll figure out a way to help them move on. One step at a time."

"I guess." I still feel bad, like I'm not doing enough. It is always so easy to feel guilty. I don't know if that will ever stop, but this feels important. It feels big, bigger than me. How many people wanted and wished for an opportunity like this? And I'm just wasting it. But Jaeli is right, what could I actually do that isn't incredibly overwhelming? Find Maggie's kid? Write to Will? I don't even know these people's last names. Let alone where they were from. Or when! Mae definitely wasn't from this time. Maybe not Neil either. Or the others I've been dreaming about every night since I started to understand. Hattie, Rafa, Maeve... my mind is a rotating door of other people's lives. I have no clue where to start. "I understand what you're saying. I guess I just want to give them something. Let them know I can hear them. Help in some way. I don't know."

"Give your shadow a reason to follow you?" I roll my eyes and Jaeli smiles into her mug. "I think Olli might be able to help you more on that front. His grandmother used to tell their stories as lessons. From what he tells me, she would pass on their problems as reasons to be honest and open and never give up hope. That's what he tries to show in his paintings and sculptures. A lot of people see them as dark, but I think they highlight that last moment where everything went wrong. Where if the person had just trusted someone, or maybe themselves, things could have been so different. Everything could have set itself right. You can let these shadows be your anchor, Livia, let them stabilize your life and put your emotions into perspective."

I'm stuck in my head for a moment, staring out the window through the leaves finally starting to turn in the late fall breeze, seeing only fragmented sections of the street. Just pieces of the passersby flitting in and out of my vision. Maybe I don't need to do everything. Maybe I *could* just put pieces out there. Help others before they became trapped under the veil.

Trust myself.

"Stories, huh?"

Jaeli smiles, the pride wafting off her in tangible waves. "Live."

"What?" I ask, reacting to what I think is my nickname.

"Live, Livia. Breathe. Everything doesn't need to happen and work perfectly all at once."

Chapter Twenty

"So you're going to give up. You're just going to put everything you've worked for this year aside and let yourself give into these delusions?" Anger boils inside me at the sight of Dr. Baron's dead stare. I have no idea how I've lasted in this office for so long. How I could have been so naive as to think someone like this could help me.

"They might not be a reality to you, but they are real to me." I throw the doctor's words back at her. "I feel like I need this. I need to tell their stories. They're important and relatable. They could save someone's life. They need to be heard."

"I'm going to need to report this. Choosing not to take the medications was one thing-"

"I am taking the medication! They aren't doing anything!" I snap. How many times do I have to repeat myself? For all the scribbling Dr. Baron did, she didn't seem to write down anything of importance. But god help her if she didn't remember my faults during times when the darkness was too much to make good and healthy decisions with my meds!

"And you're still hallucinating." The psychiatrist continued. "I didn't report you before as you were willing to work on things and of no danger to yourself. But now you want to leave therapy. That's not a healthy or well thought out decision Livia."

But it is the best decision, I think to myself. "I don't care. I'm leaving. You and the hospital. I can't do this, be here, anymore. This environment isn't good for me. It's something you should have realized ages ago even if I couldn't. I'm moving on for the better." Jaelie had seen it right away. Only two sessions in and she was guiding me to think about working somewhere else where people might understand and accept my struggle with anxiety and depression. She thinks somewhere with less stress might benefit me right now. Like maybe the coffee shop since I liked it so much and was so comfortable with Gage. She mentioned getting a roommate to help with the rent and the loneliness. Travel. Writing. I feel suffocated here suddenly. I stand up and snatch my coat off the most uncomfortable couch to ever exist.

"For what, Livia? Do you have a plan? You help people here, you have an income." Dr. Baron looks utterly baffled, like life is weighed by the money in the bank and emotion has nothing to do with it. I wonder if Nick ever had a therapist and if they fed him that same bullshit. Maybe that's what people with money really think. I don't think I would ever know, and I'm ok with that. How did someone like this even become a therapist? "Only a life lived for others is a life worthwhile."

I would believe it if Jaeli were speaking the words. Hell, if anyone else were. Coming out of Dr. Baron's mouth, they were as dry and recited as anything else. "Where'd you get that, a fortune cookie?"

Dr. Baron sneered, holier than thou, "Albert Einstein." Of course. A source of logic, not caring.

"Well, I *will* be living for others. It's in a way you might not be able to understand, but that is exactly what I'll be doing. And I'd like to start today." I put on my coat as I head for the door, Manny slowly moving from the corner to follow. I turn on my heel, I've always liked that expression. I never really understood it until this moment had my head spinning with endorphins. "Oh, and I will be continuing therapy. Elsewhere." I slam the door against any further protests and almost make it out of the building before seeing a young man picking at a barely there scar on his wrist. Manny stops too and hovers right near him, something about his silent stillness screams for attention. "Hey. You here for Elizabeth Baron?" I ask. The kid looks like he would give anything to have me stop talking. I fish around in my black hole of a bag and pull out Jaeli's card. "I know she's a little further out, but I promise she's worth it. This one." I couldn't do anything but shake my head. The kid seems to understand. He stays in his seat, but at least the card was carefully pulled from my fingers.

"Thanks." He says in a small, quiet voice. Manny squeezes my arm as I walk by and stays behind without me. The static dances over the hairs on my arm in his absence.

Hopefully they'd both be alright.

CHAPTER TWENTY ONE

"I don't think I've been bowling since a birthday party when I was like... eight." Noah breathes with a roll of his eyes. He shakes his head, returning his concentration back on the center of the lane as he throws the neon green and black ball forward. It coasts steadily at an angle until finally dropping into the left gutter. Noah grunts, his head thrown back and chuckles darkly at himself. "Jesus, I'm horrible at this."

"Maybe you should try it like that guy." I wink, thumbing over my shoulder to a probably-six year old swinging the ball forward from between his legs. "He seems to be doing pretty well." I giggle at his scowl and pick up my own bright blue ball, hurling it forward. It isn't perfect, but at least I'm consistently taking down some pins. I bring back my second ball and almost fall on my face when something stops me from swinging it forward. Noah laughs behind me, the sneaky bastard had grabbed it right off my fingers. "Cute." I snark.

"Just trying to even up the odds!" I grab another ball and send it down the lane for a split. I do an exaggerated happy dance, trying to brighten his mood further. It's working on me a little too.

I watch him slide over the line on his next throw, but it still doesn't help. It's like his ball has a magnet inside of it for that same spot in the gutter. I bite my lip trying not to smile when he whips around to look at me as if he could sense my inner mocking.

Suddenly, I get that feeling again. That everything is right with the world and I am so close to knowing what happiness feels like again, and then, it's just wrong.

Red lights flicker over Noah's face with the music and I can't help but be reminded of my dreams with Manny in the desert. Of smoke and flashes and bangs. A bowling ball hits its lane with a sharp crack that makes me jump. "I'm going to grab a drink. Want anything?" I ask a little too quickly, needing to walk off the sudden nerves.

"Nah. But I'm going to ruin your score while you're gone." I don't doubt it, but I'm not going to argue with the grin he throws my way.

"Ass." I say fondly. "I hope you get your first strike!" It's nice to see him so relaxed, the worry lines smoothed away and his face looking, maybe not as young as it should, but far better than in the harsh light of the hospital. I'm glad I had confiscated his phone at the beginning of the night. Without the weight of it glued to his hand, he seemed to let go a little. At least just enough to enjoy himself and forget for a while.

I head over to the snack counter and flinch at the spark that lights my fingers as I touch it. I should have known. I look to my right to see Vader there beside me. It wasn't usually so easy for him to sneak up on me, what with the constant whooshes and clicks. I check for anyone who might overhear before opening my mouth to scold him, but something stops me.

It was quiet.

Obviously not quiet in the bowling alley with music videos blasting, a pool game ten feet away with rowdy frat boys, and the constant barrage of heavy polyurethane meeting polished wood and pins. But Vader is quiet. Standing still as a statue, no imitation of life today. Something isn't right.

I check that Noah is still concentrating on sending balls into the gutter for me before gesturing at the shadow to follow me to the little alcove by the ladies room. It does.

Instinct takes over, something that doesn't have me afraid at the thought of touching these beings. Something that has been steadily building since I first burst out at this horribly terrifying creature and shouted *stop*, and it listened.

I raise my hand and close my fingers around the wispy veil enveloping him, the threads clinging and shifting like spider webs in the wind at my touch. I pull, and I see him, the shadow. I see Sam.

"Shit. How? When? Are you, oh god, we have to tell your brother-" My next thought is cut off at a shrill ring nearby. I peek out of the little hallway we had tucked ourselves into and see Noah dropping a ball and running to where I had left my purse. *"Shit."*

I bolt towards him.

"Hello– yes... Yes this is he. What's happened? Is he awake?..."

"Noah, wait-" Noah raises a hand in my face to stop whatever I'm about to say, brow heavy and listening intently to the phone over the bowling alley din.

"What do you mean, crashed?"

"Noah-" My voice breaks around the threat of tears. Forget Sam, his brother was crashing right in front of me.

"Hold on Liv!" He shouts. "No. that's, you have to... *he has a living will!* I did the paperwork, it was approved by the judge. You can't just stop! You have to keep trying-"

"Noah" I try again. I feel my insides cracking, the hope at saving him spilling out of me and circling the drain. I've failed.

"No, I'm coming in right now. Try again... *I said try again!* I swear to God, I will sue you for everything you're worth." He is kicking away the rented shoes and taking off with his sneakers still in his hand.

"Noah please," I grab him by the arm, jolting him to a stop. "Sam's here, Noah. Please. Just slow down."

"What?"

"Sam. He's... I think he's one of them. Has been all this time, Vader, *Dickwad,* he–"

Noah rips away from me. "You have no idea what you're talking about. You're fucking *crazy* Livia. Alright? Happy? Get away from me! Sam needs me."

"Yes he does. He's right here, just... just listen! Maybe I can get a message or-"

"Stop! Just, stop! Stop with this attention whore bullshit. Ok? Get out of my way. I never should have listened to you. I never should have left him alone." He storms off, pushing past the college students and families staring at the free entertainment in the form of their breakdown. I run back to get my shoes and purse, picking up Noah's discarded rentals along the way and shoving them at a confused looking clerk while shucking off my own and leaving those too.

"Noah wait!" I call, trying to shove high tops on my feet while running down the block after him. He speeds up at my voice. I could see that the animalistic side of Sam's shadow was a family trait now. I don't even know if he knows his way back, he is just charging forward, completely unprepared for the anguish that is waiting for him. Trapped in denial and grief and pain. I can see it in every sharp line of his body as he pushes himself down the street and I feel the leftover quakes of it in my bones from what happened with Nick on the night he hung himself. Still. I have to help. Have to stop him. That's the whole point of this disaster, isn't it? I have to be there for him. Why won't he let me? "Taxi!" I screech at a passing cab with its light on. "Noah! Please get in. It'll be faster. I'll pay, just please." I open the door and slide in, telling the cabby to wait for my friend, that we need to get to John Adams.

"Get out." Noah says from the open door."

"Noah, please just let me make sure you get there safe. Okay? Please." He will give me a look I never want to see on his face again, one that will haunt me for a long time. Dark and empty and full of hatred. He sits down hard and slams the door behind him, ignoring the perturbed cabby and grinding his teeth loud enough for me to hear.

It's a tense and silent ride. The only noise being the safety video clips on the little screen keeping count of our fare and miles for us. When we finally pull up to the entrance, I direct the driver as close as he can get to where we need to be. Noah pushes his way out of the cab and slams the door behind him again. I throw a twenty forward, not having it in me to care that the tip is ridiculous and follow him out.

"No." He turns to snap at me. It stops me dead in my tracks. I'm making this worse for him. I always make everything worse. I nod and watch him walk away, getting his bearings before charging off to berate some poor night nurse. Sam appears next to me again, I look at him, his features back under the veil but still quiet.

"You need to go be with him, I think." I whisper. "I tried to stop it, but maybe he'll be able to see you now. Maybe you can give him your message yourself. I'm sorry." The tears that have been stubbornly pinching my throat but refusing to fall finally overwhelm my eyes as I turn my back on the hospital. It isn't mine anymore.

I watch the taxi's brake lights glowing as the driver waits to pull into traffic at the other end of the parking lot. I might be able to catch him, but I think the cold night air suits me better.

I need to talk to someone. Of course today is the day I decide to walk out on my therapist. Not that Dr. Baron would have answered the phone this late at night anyway. And I don't want to bother Jaeli so soon after starting with her. Don't want to seem needy so early on. What if she is just as unreliable as Dr. Baron? And what could she really do from an hour away anyway?

I try my mother but it goes straight to voicemail. It isn't until my father's phone does the same that I remember their annual anniversary cruise to relive their honeymoon. Ted is a dead end too, but that is no surprise considering our recent exchanges. I could try Courtney, but I'm almost certain this is her weekend on call. I refuse to ruin anyone else's night tonight.

I'm wiping my wet face a block west of my walk home before I realize my feet have taken me on a detour to pass the café without my permission.

I don't know what to do. I know it's a bad idea, but I call him. It rings twice before going to voicemail, ignored. I can't bring myself to say anything. I don't even know why I had tried.

Soon enough I'm at the Grind House and almost relieved. A mess or not, I could really use one of Gage's laughs tickling my ears and something with too many calories to think about.

When I finally make it to the door, it's just in time to see my favorite baker's back turned towards me, heading over to his mop after turning the sign over to 'closed'.

I stand in empty silence for a few seconds, feeling utterly alone again. Something I was once familiar with but a feeling that had been slowly ebbing away over the last month or so.

My fingers tremble over my touch screen as I bite hard on my lip to stem the tears. Still, they find the familiar favorite easily enough. It's a force of habit. Not a good one according to Jaeli. Prolonging the trauma. Not giving myself room to heal. What am I going to do when faced with someone else eventually having his phone number? Yadda yadda. But I need a friend right now, even if they can't talk back. I barely hear my name on the wind over the shock that follows.

Nick's number goes right to voicemail as usual, but this time it's different.

I'm sorry, the caller you are trying to reach 'Hey! It's Nick.' Has a full message box. Please try your call again later. Good bye.

The call disconnects.

This is it.

There's no one else.

I'm so tired. So done.

CHAPTER TWENTY TWO

I slam into the apartment. I start digging through everything, looking for what Nick and Ted insisted on keeping just in case. What my brother had hidden when I was going through (what he thought was) my roughest patch. That was nothing compared to this. Eventually I find what I need hidden behind the fire extinguisher under the sink. It makes sense, he was probably thinking of things we would need in an emergency.

The weight is lighter than I remember. It makes everything easier.

Sam starts raging behind me. He grabs my shoulders when he sees it and gives me a shake. It's jarring. I can feel the spider web static clinging to my arms but even if he has a face now, he's not really here. He should have stayed at the hospital with his brother. I'm certain I've failed Noah and that he would be able to see Sam and the other shadows now. Guilt roils my stomach but I can't help the thought of *good* from crossing my mind. Maybe he'll end up believing me after all.

I'm pulled out of my dark thoughts by a voice, one I am hearing for the first time. It was different than I imagined when Noah had talked about his brother or when I had chatted with Sam while checking up on him. But I'm certain it is him. The voice gives me a message, begging me to try one more time. I do kind of owe him, especially if I am abandoning all of them now. He lets go of my arms to let me drag the phone out of my pocket, impossibly heavier than the gun. I call Noah one more time.

Sam looks like his heart would break if it were still beating when I put the automated voice on speaker and give the phone a sarcastic shake. Still, I owe it to at least one of them. I leave his message.

I drop the phone down on the counter and go to my bedroom. Sam follows, he is silent, just staring at me. I pull out the lighter and listen to the scrape, watch the sparks as the rusty wheel fails to ignite what little oil is left, if any. I try to spark something in myself with it. My tears are drying, I have finally gone numb. That of all things is what pushes me over the edge.

I had wanted to be numb so badly when all of this had started. When Nick screamed at me, was so disappointed in me, when I broke his heart because of it. When he died. I hadn't wanted to feel it when Ted moved out or when he gave up on me after the ghosts invaded. Of course, now that I want to feel something, anything but the darkness and guilt and regret, I go numb.

I have never really needed the talk down before. I had been curious, mostly, because it felt like death was all around me and I couldn't understand what pushed Nick into it. Now I can see the difference between walking out to the ledge and just looking over into the dark and wondering what it would be like to jump, what I would miss, what I wouldn't have to deal with. And walking out to the ledge and not caring anymore about anything. I can see the relief in the pain and empty dark heading my way as the wind would rush my face. Imagining the fall and not the effect. There's a selfishness there and a selflessness. For how could you be selfish if you don't even exist? If you don't even know yourself or have a self to know. If you're truly nothing to the people around you, and make yourself nonexistent, then why would anyone be effected? How?

It's different now. I can clearly see Nick's motivation and relate. I want that same calm and peace. Somehow my hands are still shaking. And even though my mind is thoroughly made up, there is still that niggling sensation of guilt.

Guilt.

I would probably be one of them.

Jaeli is right. They are my anchor. But not the kind that stabilizes. They don't give me purpose. They are here to pull me down.

One of us. One of us, my mind supplies.

Maybe it's better to live through someone else. Maybe that's all they are. Not creatures, or ghosts or tormented souls or demons or boogie men. Just selfless people latching onto the closest thing to a self that they know. Another selfless person. That doesn't seem so bad. Maybe some people just aren't meant to live as long as they do. Maybe they serve their purpose and can't find another one in life. Maybe ending it for themselves is their end. You know? If everything happens for a reason? I think to myself, watching my hands tremble around the gun laid across my palms. *"What, were you one of those hippie philosophy girls? I could see that."* I remember Courtney asking from that night. I look to Sam, still vibrating with rage and I reach out to touch him, to see his face. Not bruised beyond recognition like when he first arrived at the hospital or thin and pale as he was when we left him in bed to go bowling. Young and smooth, with early twentysomething baby fat on his freshly shaven cheeks. "You're here because maybe something happened to you that shouldn't have. But Nick's not. He's not here. He killed himself and he's not a shadow. Maybe it is the right choice for some people. Maybe I should. I never got to tell him anything. He just assumed that my saying I needed to think about it was my answer. I never got to tell him that I loved him. That maybe love was like a best friend, but that I needed time to know if that's the kind of love I wanted. That I wanted to take things slow, and talk about his anger, and help him. But that mostly I just wanted my best friend back.

"Some people do want to marry their best friends. Some people do want to spend the rest of their life with their best friend. I just needed time to figure out if that was what I wanted. Why didn't he wait?" I start crying again, start to feel again. I let my hand drop from Sam's face to cradle the gun, to yell at it as if it were Nick, the only ghost I *wanted* to haunt me. I let myself process the grief and confusion for the first time. I let myself get angry.

"Damn it Nick! You were always so selfish! Always so controlling! *Do this, don't do that! My way or the highway! It was my goddamn life!*"

I straighten the gun again, clicking back the hammer and looking right into the deep darkness of the barrel. "Well fuck you. Maybe we weren't best friends. Maybe I meant nothing at all. Maybe he wasn't supposed to. Maybe I am." Sam slowly sits. His arm extends as if he's reaching over, trying to envelope me in more darkness. "Yeah. Maybe I should."

I place my thumb over the trigger, stroking its curve. It's a different angle than I am used to. I had been to the range with Ted three times before he gave up on me. My aim was horrific, probably my stance too. Not a single bullet on the target sheet. I remember laughing, feeling almost proud that even with a deadly weapon I wouldn't be able to hurt anyone. It had frustrated the hell out of him.

I am pretty sure I can hit this target. I'm frozen in time, staring down the dark tunnel of the gun's barrel, heart racing to a panic. I feel the static of a ghostly hand on my shoulder. An overwhelming sense of *regret* fills me and in the same instant I hear the bang. I remember a full bodied twitch like waking up from a nightmare and then a light.

The gun falls to the floor.

CHAPTER TWENTY THREE

Gage is remembering the bad times when he turns his sign over to 'closed' for the night. "Gotta fake it til you make it," he sighs under his breath, punctuating it with a laugh that doesn't feel as merry as it sounds. He pasted on a smile day after day until his laugh felt real again and everything else started to come together around it. He sold the guts of his great aunt's cherished book store that had been failing without her passion and opened Grind House. He hopes she's proud he's doing something he is passionate about and doesn't want vengeance on her books scattered across the very internet that she claimed would be the death of the store. It had been a rough day, but he still loves this place. Loves his work and the people that now surround him, he only wishes they would stick around to help with the cleanup.

Gage is scrubbing a stubborn caramel stain when he feels someone behind him. He turns to see Livia at the door. That's exactly what this day needs—a little bit of her sunshine to break up his own personal rain cloud. But she's running away. That hasn't happened in a while.

"Livia! Liv! Hey." She's gone. And obviously upset. He remembers the closed sign. "Shit."

He gives up on the sticky mess and does the bare minimum to close up safely before locking the door behind him.

He takes the long way around. He's not one hundred percent sure where she lives. He's not a creep. He just wants to make sure she gets home safe and if he were ever to bump into her then, hey what a coincidence! And then they could talk and maybe he would have the courage to do more than give her free food he didn't think she was even eating.

He may have told himself he wasn't a creep one or two times before because he knows her block like it's his own. But not her apartment! That's not too bad, right?

Yeah. He was a creep.

"God I suck."

*****

Courtney is working late. Again. The third time this week she's been locked in because of fucking Darleen. She loves her job, but there is a breaking point and she has reached it. She's finally on her way to punch out for a quick fifteen when a familiar brooding brother tries to slam a hydraulic door in her face and continues on his path of destruction down the hall until confronted by Kim Bishop from intensive care. That's not good.

She makes her way to her locker and digs around for her phone. She doesn't even know where to begin with this one. The call goes to voicemail and she rolls her eyes. Typical Livia.

"Hey, I know you and the Marsh brother are close. You know I'm not supposed to be saying any of this, but fuck it. I like you two together. It's your patient I think. His brother could really use you right now. If he keeps up the way he's going they're going to kick him out. Okay? Call him. Now. Talk to you later."

Courtney thumbs the red button to hang up and feels like it was nowhere near enough. She wishes Livia would just talk to her like the old days.

*****

Ted sighs deeply, content and warm and the happiest he has been in a long time.

It had officially been the worst day of proposals ever. EVER. Seriously. What could go wrong did go wrong.

Fenway Park : Ted was by himself inside a giant heart on the big screens because Hannah had gone to the bathroom.

Hannah's favorite Restaurant : Closed! Indefinitely. And they had no idea until after he had suggested gnocchi and mascarpone cheesecake from the place and drove all the way there. He couldn't let himself propose over the frozen chewy hell that was their replacement lunch at the classy looking restaurant across the street. Ambiance, five stars. Microwavable breakfast sausage over pasta instead of the Italian links promised on the menu, instant zero star yelp review.

Take her to the wharf at sunset? : Would have been a great idea if she wasn't running a mile ahead of him to get back to the car and out of the frigid wind.

Finally they're back in the car and warming their hands in front of the heater and leaning in for a kiss when his phone alarm goes off. And *shit,* he remembers he was supposed to pick up his parent's dogs while they were on vacation. By the time he gets to his parents' house, it is pretty much guaranteed the dogs will have peed all over the place. And when he opens the door after the long drive, the smell that greets him proves it isn't just pee.

When they've fulfilled the incredibly unromantic duty of cleaning up a river of Great Dane piss and the horrifying task of pulling paper towel lengths out of the anxiety eater Pomeranian's ass, he gets a phone call. One he really doesn't need at the moment. He couldn't even help himself today. He vocally ignores it, much to Hannah's disappointment. He turns the damn phone off and puts a smile back on her face with a hot shower.

It had been a hell of a day. But he can't complain laying here in his much too small childhood bed with the woman of his dreams.

"Didn't your sister call?"

"Mhm. Two more minutes." He smiles into her neck, lifting her hand to see the ring two sizes too small balancing above the knuckle of her ring finger.

She laughs and pulls her hand back, already in the habit of playing with the band. She's adorable. "Jerk." And far too good for him.

Ted rolls his eyes, "Fine."

When he turns the phone back on there's a voicemail. Not uncommon these days, but he lifts the phone to listen to it and sticks his tongue out at his fiancé (Jesus his heart beats double time just thinking the word) for good measure.

"Ted? Teddy! What?" His face must have betrayed his shock.

He shoots out of bed, throwing the phone back to Hannah because he doesn't have words for that. "Livia. I think she's done something. I have to go."

"Let me come with you." He really does love her. They scramble for clothes while Ted calls on repeat.

"Come on Liv. Pick up Damnit!" There's a click and Ted freezes in the doorway. "Livia-"

"No, this is Noah" says a tight voice. Ted knows that tone if not the man. His knees buckle.

*****

Noah is leaving the morgue when he turns his phone back on. He doesn't know what to do, where to go.

Sam is dead.

His brother is dead and his chest is tight and he is completely alone. His whole body aches, his legs are shaking. He has never been so tired in his life and he thinks he may pass out before he knows where he's going.

When the phone finally turns back on, it starts vibrating and chiming with missed calls and messages. Livia. He was such an ass. Some small part of him knows it isn't her fault, that she couldn't have known how tired his brother's lungs were. He knows that she had just been trying to cheer him up.

Still, if it wasn't for her meddling in their life, he would have been with Sam when it happened. He could have made the doctors keep trying. Could have done... something. Maybe. He walks out to the angry looks of people annoyed by his noise and sits on the bench outside with his head in his hands.

He can't go home. Doesn't know if he would ever be able to. To look around at the life they had tried to carve out for themselves and know he is truly alone. He wipes a hand down his face, feeling guilty for so many reasons, but mostly for thinking about himself when his brother is dead.

He looks down at the phone and decides listening to the messages can't be the worst thing for him. At least then he would know if she got home safe even if he didn't want to talk to her just yet.

The first message is just a few seconds of wind and street noise. The second message has rage flooding through him before everything around him freezes. Even his heart feels like it has stopped between beats.

"Noah I have a message from Sam. I know you're about to hang up but this is his only shot to say it. I'm... I'm done. With everything. Okay? So just listen! He says it's not your fault. That he made his own choices because it wasn't fair to constantly be depending on you for everything. That it wasn't fair to either of you. He didn't think you would listen. So, for proof I guess, he said you had a dog named Wiggles when he was four and that the dog would freak out when people left the house and one day you got home from school and he had jumped out the window.

"He said he found out about Santa because you were supposed to be watching him when he was sick but you let him go to your mom for help and he saw her wrapping the presents. The same presents Santa left a couple days later. He said the lighter wasn't yours. It was in his pocket when you found him. That mom gave it to Sam because he was always a little messed up.

"He says he knows you lit it every night for him and sometimes during the day too. It's empty now. I'll leave it with a note for you just in case you want it back. Alright? So he doesn't blame you. Get your head out of your ass and start living for yourself for once in your damn life. His words, not mine. But he's right. Good luck. I'm taking an easier route. Maybe see you on the other side."

Noah holds the phone in front of him, listening to the automated voice giving him options to save, delete or call back. He listens to the voice say the message is saved and watches the phones light fade and turn to black.

How could she know that stuff? He had believed her about the shadows at first, but the more she talked about them the more he thought that maybe she just wanted attention. Especially when he got to know her a little better and saw how alone she is. But either way, she said she couldn't talk to them. So how? How did she know?

Something felt very wrong inside of him. Like he made some huge mistake that hadn't quite come around to bite him in the ass yet but that he knew was on its way. He thinks back to the message. About Livia's tone of voice. She didn't sound mad or even upset. Impatient almost?

Flat.

And then some of the things she had said...

Noah is on his feet and running so fast it makes him dizzy. He hopes he remembers the way, but even when his mind falters on what turns to take, his feet don't slow.

He's mad again. Furious. They needed to talk. Even if it was just to tell her to fuck off, that he never wanted to hear her voice again. But he knew it was more, that he was scared. That he never wanted to hear her voice sound like *that* ever again.

He almost runs right by the apartment, matching all the others with the window bars. What had him stop short was his gut clenching in relief. Noah swears he sees Sam for a second. Just a second. But it's enough. Something he would have given anything for and needs to see desperately again once the grief washes back over him in a fresh wave at remembering it couldn't have been him.

He runs up the three flights of stairs to her door and slams his fist against it. Banging as hard as he can. He tries to open it but it doesn't budge and he hears nothing from inside. Noah runs back to the street to check the windows again. He sees a familiar face heading his way with a flashlight from across the street and runs over to nab it, screaming that it's important.

"What the hell?" The guy shouts, following him. "Wait, aren't you-"

He can't be bothered with small talk right now. Something is wrong and ghosts might just be real. "Livia!" Noah screams. If he had faith in his ability to break down the door, it would be in splinters already. He shines the light up into what he thinks is Livia's bedroom window, flashing it back and forth. If she's in there, she can't miss it. "Liv! Livia!" He's screaming his voice raw. "Damnit Livia, open the door! Please! I'm sorry! I believe you, please!"

He hears a voice next to him, just like Sam's and it shocks him just as he's about to sacrifice his shoulder against the door and deadbolt. "Good choice idiot." Noah stops dead, the tears he's been hiding behind the rage burst forth. His throat burns and he almost misses the sound from in the building, throwing himself back inside and up the stairs. The man, the laughing baker, is hot on his trail. The second he sees Livia looking terrified in the doorway he throws himself into her arms and cries. He hasn't let himself do this since he was a little kid, crying over Wiggles, but god it feels good. He's never letting her go again.

"It's not your fault." Noah breathes hard into her neck as she shakes in his arms. "I believe you, I'm sorry. I believe you." She clings just as hard, mumbling her own apologies into his hair.

"Uh, I hate to interrupt... whatever this is, but can I get that light back? I'm just, I just wanted to make sure you were okay and you are. So I'm just gunna go." Gage gestures with his thumb motioning behind him but as he reaches for the flashlight Livia darts her arm out and snatches the poor guy. He smells like coffee and vanilla frosting and Noah can't seem to care that he's sandwiched between the two of them. He can't help but feel touch starved as the guy sighs and gives into the hugging. "Well, this is not how I imagined our first *embrace* but I should have known you were weird when you kept coming to a café for tap water."

Livia is shaking when he lets her go. He hears her phone going off again and again from inside the apartment and can't stand the thought of someone else feeling the unbelievable worry he had been a minute ago. Besides, he thinks he's left her in good hands with perfect laugh man. Noah finds the glow of the phone on her kitchen counter and swipes the screen to answer.

"Livia?" A man yells, anger and worry blasting through his eardrums. He knows that tone, had perfected it himself. This must be the brother.

He sniffs away the emotion and tries to keep his voice calm as he answers. "No, this is Noah." He takes another breath when he sees the gun on the floor of the little hallway. He picks it up, the metal still warm from Livia's hands. The emotion clogs his throat again as he tries to smooth things over. "It's ok. Livia's okay. But she almost wasn't. Take it from one big brother to another, you need to get here. Now. You two need to talk."

EPILOGUE

It was the laugh I think to myself.

I smooth my hands over the shiny silver of my Best Maid's dress. I'm sitting next to Gage and across from Noah who is next to a girl from my writing group that I set him up with a few months ago. There are a couple shadows in the room, one seems to be attached to the banquet hall itself. The other is hovering by the bar or rather the day drinker glued to it. They don't notice me yet, but I'm sure at least one will be following me home tonight to tell me their story like all the others.

Gage is laughing at the Maid of Honor's speech about growing up with Hannah, his arm slung around me, gripping tighter as he shakes with good humor. It makes me glow, his light filling in all the places that still ache inside of me with love and that beautiful sound of his full bodied laughter. I breathe in the light and let it push out the darkness in my heart. It's an invigorating recharge.

For the first time in forever, I remember what being happy feels like and can actually admit to feeling it grow inside me. There are still dark days of course, hills to climb and pills to take, but life is balanced again. Memories aren't as terrifying and going to bed at night is relaxing and enjoyed instead of just being preparation for the battle of the next day.

There's still a broken lighter on my night stand and a stain on the carpet that meets the kitchen linoleum, but it's covered by a brightly painted end table with a single candle and a picture from my college days with Nick and Ted. It sits right next to a picture from a carnival showing me screaming my heart out next to Gage while he holds onto me for dear life as Noah laughs behind us, clutching his belly and probably accidently eating some of my hair.

Life goes on, and even the days where I feel trapped in the shadow of my past, I know that if I reach out there will be my choice of hands to hold reaching back.

About the Author

This Rhode Island native has wanted to be a storyteller since hearing her first bedtime fairytale. She asked for a word processor for Christmas at age four and has kept her promise to Santa by writing every day since.

Her first series of books has been set in motion with the hope of making mental illness a more readily accessible topic. She writes characters with mental illness as the heroes with the goal that more people will see themselves as worthwhile individuals and no longer just horror movie villains.

Emily's love of the supernatural, science fiction, and fantasy will surely be explored in later works of fiction, romance, and children's books.

Stay tuned at *www.emilytallman.com*

Made in the USA
Columbia, SC
27 June 2018